DALTON'S VALLEY

DALTON'S VALLEY

by

Ed Law

Dales Large Print Books
Long Preston, North Yorkshire,
BD23 4ND, England.

British Library Cataloguing in Publication Data.

Law, Ed
    Dalton's valley.

    A catalogue record of this book is
    available from the British Library

    ISBN   978-1-84262-596-5 pbk

First published in Great Britain in 2007 by Robert Hale Limited

Copyright © Ed Law 2007

Cover illustration © Gordon Crabb by arrangement with
Alison Eldred

Published in Large Print 2008 by arrangement with
Robert Hale Limited

Dales Large Print is an imprint of Library Magna Books Ltd.

Printed and bound in Great Britain by
T.J. (International) Ltd., Cornwall, PL28 8RW

PROLOGUE

'When I give the word,' Deke Grant said, looking right then left at his fellow prisoners, 'we get 'em!'

Paul Stark and Billy Boyd grunted their approval, the patter of the pounding rain making their words inaudible, then settled down on to their haunches with their backs against the wet bars to await developments. They had waited for ten long days for just such an opportunity as this one and it was unlikely they'd get a better chance.

The mobile barred cage in which they were prisoners had been trundling along, every turn of the wheels taking them further away from Durando and closer to White Falls and their inevitable demise.

Trailing behind and ahead of them were a dozen guards led by the indomitable Sheriff Rory Blake, a man who viewed it as his singular duty to watch his prisoners' every movement.

Inside the cage Deke and Paul had rarely spoken, circumstance having put together two men who would never naturally associate with the other. Both men had spoken even more rarely with the third member Billy, a callow youth of seventeen.

But with all three men sharing a desperate desire to escape, they'd kept a constant vigil, awaiting a lucky break that would let them capitalize on their first stroke of luck. It had happened on the night when Billy had been captured. A guard had beaten him and Billy had collapsed under the onslaught, but as he'd fallen his flailing hand had caught hold of the guard's clothing and dislodged a spare cell key.

The guard hadn't noticed and so Billy had gathered up the key. Throughout the remainder of his beating he'd kept his hand tightly closed. Then with steely determination he'd guarded his secret while the three men had awaited the opportunity to use it.

And now that opportunity had arrived.

'Where in tarnation are they?' the guard Orson Malloy demanded, peering over his shoulder through the torrent of rainfall.

'Those trees cut them off,' another guard shouted, dragging his horse away from the edge of the slope. Towering pines were to his left and to his right there was a gaping expanse of night-blackness, proof that they

8

were high up and that the hill down which they had been zig-zagging angled away sharply. 'Rory's stuck back there.'

'Then go help him,' Orson said. A lightning flash etched his form in sharp relief and showed him pointing up the slope. 'You men, get down off those horses and watch the prisoners.'

Inside the cell, Deke grinned as Orson again reduced the number of men guarding them. A sudden flood had surged by dragging a sprawling mass of fallen trees and mud across the trail and cutting off six men from the mobile cell. Now with another guard heading away to try to help Rory and the others, only five men were left to actively guard them.

'Hey,' Deke shouted, holding out a hand to cup the teeming water, 'we're drowning in here.'

As thunder boomed out, Orson drew his horse up to the cell and considered him through the bars with his usual surly glare.

'You can't drown in an open cell, unfortunately.'

Deke chuckled. 'You could be right, but the kid ain't looking good. The cold is killing him.'

Orson darted his gaze past Deke to

consider Billy, who took this as his cue to keel over on to his side and start coughing. Billy delivered his coughs in a manner that was so unconvincing Orson merely grunted and turned to move away, but when Billy continued to cough, he shouted at him to be quiet. Billy delivered another racking cough and then another.

The rain continued to plummet down, pattering so heavily off the ground it splattered arcs of mud against Orson's legs, the hammering noise on the cell floor was deafening, and through it all Billy continued to cough. In irritation, Orson climbed down from his horse and jumped on to the back of the wagon on which the cell stood and peered through the cell door at the hunched prisoners within.

'Be quiet!' he demanded.

Billy coughed again, a spasm racking his body. Then he rolled to the side to lie against the bars. The opportunity was too great for Orson to resist and he delivered a kick through the bars into Billy's stomach, another lightning flash providing a frozen mask-like vision of Billy's open-mouthed and pained face. Billy bleated, then coughed again and this encouraged Orson to kick him again.

'Leave him alone,' Paul said. 'We're all cold.'

Pleas for clemency was a sure-fire way of goading the guards into continuing a beating and so, to deliver a huge kick into Billy's ribs, Orson pressed himself to the bars and positioned himself carefully. He swung back his leg then thrust it forward in a savage arc that would be sure to splinter bones, but it never reached its target.

Billy rolled away as thunder roared and Deke surged to his feet. He thrust a huge arm through the bars and wrapped it around Orson's neck then dragged him back against the bars. Two weeks of pent-up anger fuelled his vice-like grip and before any of the other guards could react a sickening crack sounded as the burly Deke snapped his neck like a twig.

Orson slumped in Deke's grip as, with a level of teamwork only mutual desperation can create, Paul grabbed Orson's gun through the bars and Billy ran for the door, the key now displayed for all to see. He slammed it into the lock, which sprang. The door screeched open and in moments all three men piled out to stand on the edge of the wooden wagon.

A gunshot from the nearest guard scythed

into the bars and whistled away before Deke leapt from the back of the wagon and slammed into him. The two men went down in the mud, rolling over each other as they struggled.

Billy moved to follow Deke from the wagon, but Paul grabbed his arm and bade him to keep his head down. Billy instantly appreciated this request when the remaining guards got their wits about them and splayed gunfire at them.

Paul chose his moment then risked bobbing up to return gunfire, but in the driving rain he found it hard to pick his targets and he soon dropped down. A muffled gunshot sounded. The guard on top of Deke bucked then rolled away and when Deke came to his feet he had the guard's gun in hand. He crouched down and with deadly speed hammered lead.

Encouraged and emboldened now, Paul jumped down from the wagon to join him and the two men fired as one. Cries of pain went up as one then another guard paid for the weeks of torment they'd inflicted on these men.

'Is that the last?' Deke shouted as another man ploughed face first into the mud.

'There were just five men left here,' Billy

said, joining them, 'and you got 'em all.'

A maniacal grin crossed Deke's features while Paul patted Billy's back.

'With your help, kid. We couldn't have got away without you.'

'Quit the talk,' Deke muttered. 'We ain't free yet, and Rory ain't far away.'

This comment spurred the men into action and they hurried around the mobile cell, heading for the horses. They didn't get to within ten feet of the nearest before Deke's worst fears materialized.

Rory and the remaining guards emerged from the driving rain, riding in close formation, and laid down such a barrage of gunfire that the escapees could do nothing but flee for their lives. They rounded the wagon with lead peppering splinters at their backs as they dived for cover. Unfortunately, that cover was on the other side of the wagon to the horses. Worse, a quick assessment of their situation revealed that between them they had three bullets and were facing seven men. They would have to brave crossing to one of the bodies to get a gunbelt, or risk going for the horses.

Deke reckoned they should get more bullets and Paul reckoned they should go for the horses, but Billy suggested they could do both. So on the count of three, acting before Rory could reach a defendable location, they surged out and charged around the wagon. Billy and Paul ran for the horses while Deke headed for the guard with the broken neck.

They might have succeeded, but the one factor none of them had considered curtailed their plans. The rain had converted the high trail to an expanse of slick and sliding mud and as Billy reached a horse, he suddenly felt his stomach lurch and then he fell. A whole length of the trail gave way and all three men along with the horses and the mobile cell went tumbling down the slope, plummeting headlong into the darkness.

Within seconds Rory and the guards disappeared from view as the landslide carried them off into the unknown. None of the men would have chosen this method of escape, but Deke and then Paul whooped with joy as they hurtled away.

For almost a minute they slid down the slope and when they came to a shuddering halt they were several hundred yards below their former guards. With the route above them impassable and treacherous, that few hundred yards might well have been miles.

They had fetched up beside a river, giving them a possible avenue of escape and Deke considered the river then waded through the clinging mud to the others.

'Stop wasting time,' he said. 'We can get away now.'

'*We* can,' Paul said, kneeling beside the third member of their group. 'But the kid's going nowhere. He's broken his leg.'

Deke looked down at Billy then at his right leg, which stuck out to the side with an angle no limb should have. He shrugged.

'Then leave him.'

Paul's mouth fell open in shock. 'We'd have never got away if it hadn't been for Billy. He got the key. He–'

'Talk like that won't get us away from the likes of Rory Blake. Leave him.'

'I'm not doing that,' Paul said.

Both men locked gazes until Deke swirled round, snorting in derision.

His brisk movement suggested he'd leave both of them to fend for themselves, but after three paces he stopped.

'All right,' he murmured. 'We stick together for now, but the moment the kid slows us down, we leave him.'

Paul nodded. Then both men looked up the slope. Sheriff Rory Blake, a man who would never relent from a pursuit, wasn't visible, but even so they both shivered then set about locating the horses that had travelled down with them. Several were alive and they managed to snag two. Deke also located Orson's dead body and his gunbelt.

As neither man reckoned they had enough time to construct a stretcher right now, they had no choice but to pick up the injured lad and sling him over the back of a horse.

Then they set off, broadly keeping alongside the river, their ultimate destination unknown.

CHAPTER 1

Dalton had been staring at the small rock that was lying on the river bottom for several minutes before he hunkered down beside the river, then reached into the water to grab it. Even when the rock emerged from the water it still appeared to be exactly what he thought it was – a nugget of gold, about the size of a baby's finger.

He hefted the nugget, prodded it, and even sniffed it, but only when a stray beam of sunlight illuminated it did Dalton smile. He'd never seen gold before, but he was sure this had to be the real thing.

He allowed himself a subdued chuckle of delight then tucked the rock in his pocket while he waded around, peering into the water in the hope that the nugget had some companions. But when he failed to find another nugget, a sudden worry overcame him and he stomped out on to dry land.

His former plans of fishing now forgotten, he headed past his house and upriver. A half-mile on he slipped through a rising slope of felled trees to the house of his friend Loren Steele. Loren was a resourceful and wise man who often surprised Dalton with his knowledge of obscure subjects and if anyone knew whether the rock he'd found was real gold, Loren would.

'Yup,' Loren said finally. 'It's gold all right.'

Standing outside Loren's house with the river gurgling along below them, Dalton considered Loren's firm jaw and downcast eyes. He knew Loren well and reckoned he could work out when he was joshing him, but this time he was hiding his feelings well.

'You sure?' Dalton asked. 'You don't exactly look happy.'

'I ain't.' Loren handed the nugget back to Dalton.

Dalton took it, wondering why Loren should be so grumpy about his good fortune. It wasn't like him to be jealous.

'Cheer up. I don't know nothing about gold, but there's a gold mine up in Durando, so I reckon it must have come from further upriver.' Dalton winked. 'Now you know you've got something worthwhile to look out for, you might find yourself a nugget of your own.'

Loren closed his eyes, wincing, and when

18

he opened them they were distant and sad.

'That is the one thing I could do without.'

Dalton set his hands on his hips. 'I don't understand what you mean. This has to change everything.'

Loren stared at him, but when Dalton raised his eyebrows, encouraging him to speak his mind, Loren drew him forward so that they could see along the length of the river.

Today it babbled and foamed pleasantly. Upriver the pine forest closed in and downriver Dalton's own house stood. Just in view was the settlement of Two Forks, the long-established buildings on the north side of the river standing solidly along a single track road. The more recent shacks on the south side of the river had a more sporadic pattern, but in the afternoon sunshine the whole settlement twinkled invitingly.

'Why would you want to change anything?' Loren asked. He waited, but when Dalton was unable to provide an answer he continued speaking. 'We all had different reasons for coming out here, but we all shared a common ideal of living our lives our way. Why would we want what gold can give us?'

Dalton lowered his head, ashamed that his delight in finding the nugget had made him forget this fact.

'I guess I couldn't want for nothing more, but life sure was tough last winter. I just reckoned gold might make things a bit easier for me ... for everyone.'

'And it could, but it doesn't end with one nugget.' Loren patted Dalton's shoulder then gripped it. 'That's how it started in Durando and from what I've heard that town's gone to hell. Gold does something bad to a man's soul that tears him up inside. Soon, other men will come out here searching for more gold, and they won't care whose land it's on.'

'I guess you're right.' Dalton hefted the nugget, enjoying its weight, but wishing he had the courage to fling it as far as he could. Then he reconsidered his comment that there was nothing he wanted that gold could give him and he had to admit there was something he wanted. 'But would you help me make this nugget into something – like a brooch, or a pendant?'

Loren laughed, his former ill-mood forgotten.

'Or a ring?'

Dalton couldn't help but smile. 'Now that would be something.'

'I don't reckon Eliza Boone is the sort of

woman who'd be impressed by gold trinkets,' Loren chided, although his lively eyes betrayed the fact he was joking.

'I know, and that's why I'd like to make her one.'

'Now that's sensible talking, Dalton. I'll put some thought into how we could do it.'

With Loren effectively dismissing the subject of the gold, they settled down, as was their wont on a warm afternoon, to pass a pleasant hour or so in silence, drinking coffee companionably. But Dalton's thoughts couldn't help but dwell on the nugget. So when he left Loren, he decided to see Eliza and use some gentle probing to find out whether she'd ever dreamed of owning a gold trinket.

He set off for Two Forks, the nugget weighing heavily in his pocket.

Loren had said everyone in Two Forks had had a reason to seek out a new life far from everyone else, and Dalton's reason had been more pressing than most.

Eighteen months ago he'd killed a man. His motive had been just, but the law hadn't viewed his actions that way and so he'd effectively ended his status as a wanted man by assuming a new identity and joining a group of settlers. Now, he had started his life afresh, but for him the danger of returning to heavily populated areas would always be present and living in an isolated small community such as this one was his safest option.

The settlers themselves had suffered much hardship in finding this place. Seventeen wagons and families had set out, but illness, a terrible flood, and encounters of a more human kind had decimated their ranks. Only nine families remained to trundle into this valley where they were met by an inviting and fertile spread of land at the meeting point for three rivers. By then there just weren't enough people to sustain a viable community.

But they'd had luck. Other settlers had settled down here earlier and so Two Forks was already a functioning township. Rather than start their own settlement, they'd joined these people.

Unfortunately, the newcomers had arrived late in the year; a long and harsh winter had followed and so their presence had been a burden that the original settlers could have done without. As a result they hadn't been welcomed with open arms and the unease the original settlers had felt when they'd seen nine wagons heading down the valley hadn't receded.

But on this early spring afternoon, with a gold nugget in his pocket, such concerns felt as if they were a long way behind him.

Dalton used the well-travelled path down to the south side of town, then veered off towards the small house beside the river that Eliza shared with her brother Newell. Long before he reached the house he saw that a commotion was taking place. Practically the entire inhabitants of the south side of the river had congregated outside Eliza's house, gesticulating animatedly and talking.

A twinge of concern rippled through Dalton's thoughts and he speeded up, his concern growing when he didn't see Eliza amongst the gathered people. Closer to, he noticed two people he didn't recognize. Visitors were rare and this in itself was a good enough reason for the animated activity, and Dalton would have become intrigued if he could see Eliza.

Just as he was about to break into a run, she emerged from the building, rubbing her hands on a cloth, and those hands were dirty, perhaps even blood-streaked.

'Eliza,' Dalton shouted. 'Are you all right?'

She put a cleaned hand up to her brow then acknowledged him with a brief smile of the kind that always cheered him. But he noticed her distress in the way she jerked from side to side as she slipped through the crowd. When she emerged she looked to the river, rocking from foot to foot as if she was looking out for someone.

'Have you seen Jefferson?' she asked when Dalton joined her.

'Jefferson Parker?' He watched her nod. 'I've only just arrived in town. What's wrong?'

Eliza pointed at the two newcomers. One was a thick-set bear of a man, with so much hair bristling on his arms he probably hadn't had enough hair left to cover the shining expanse of his bald head. The other man was rangy, with furtive fingers worrying his sleeves, but Dalton decided he was more worried than devious.

'We've got visitors,' she said. 'And one of them, Billy, is badly injured.'

At the mention of Billy's name the newcomers glanced their way. The rangy man had concern for this man written all over his narrowed eyes and lip-biting expression. The other man merely sneered then spat to the side.

Dalton joined Eliza in looking out for Jefferson, but already the arrival of these newcomers had caused a tremor of concern to flutter in his guts, and he didn't identify why until he saw that both men were packing guns. In a peaceful town like Two Forks where nobody needed such weaponry, that was reason enough to be concerned.

Dalton placed a hand on Eliza's shoulder.

'Don't worry,' he whispered. 'Everything will be fine.'

'I know. Jefferson will be able to help.'

Dalton was minded to mention that Jefferson wasn't the problem, but instead he looked at the newcomers. As he'd half-expected the bear-like man was already looking at him and he didn't look away when he noticed Dalton's interest, although in a casual gesture he did rest a hand on his gunbelt.

'Yeah,' Dalton said. 'Jefferson will help.'

CHAPTER 2

Jefferson Parker came traipsing through the shallow crossing-point of the river. Held high above his head was a rolled-up blanket containing the tools he'd require. At his side was a man who, from the descriptions he'd received, Dalton identified as being Milo Milton, a traveller who had arrived a few days ago from Durando, but who had since stayed on the northern side of town.

The people outside Eliza's house also espied Milo and a murmuring went up. In the six months that they'd been here they'd not met any newcomers to the valley. Yet in a matter of minutes four new people would be here.

Everyone began to speculate about why Milo was accompanying Jefferson, but now that Eliza had seen that Jefferson was coming, she slipped back into her house. Dalton didn't want to be dragged into the speculation and so after a final glance at the gun-toting strangers, he followed her inside.

The two new men outside were broadly

the same age as himself, but the injured man, Billy Boyd, was young, being nothing more than a youth. He lay on his back on the floor, staring up at the ceiling with pain and perhaps fear contorting his face into a frozen grimace. He levered himself up on to his elbows then darted his tear-streaked gaze at Dalton, but Dalton guessed what Billy wanted to know and he shook his head.

'I'm Dalton,' he said. 'Jefferson Parker is crossing the river and he'll be here in a moment.'

What should have been good news didn't cheer him and he flopped down on to his back.

'What will he say?' he asked, despair making his voice shake.

Dalton was unsure what he meant, but Eliza mouthed 'leg' to him, so he moved round to stand over Billy. A putrid whiff made Dalton wrinkle his nose. He noticed a length of reeking cloth by the fire, festering juices having set it broadly in the shape of a leg before it'd been cut away.

A fresh cloth now lay over Billy's twisted right leg. But a dark mass was already seeping through the cloth in an area beneath the knee and the putrid reek of death emerging from it told Dalton why this young man was scared and why Eliza was concerned.

'I reckon he'll say he'll help you,' Dalton said, venturing a smile. 'And he'll be here in a few minutes, so don't you worry.'

'I've done plenty of that,' Billy said, somehow returning the smile before he took long, calming breaths that didn't appear to help him.

Dalton searched for something comforting to say as Eliza went to the fire and opened up a pot to check on the heat of the water she was boiling.

'How did this happen?' Dalton asked, lost for anything else to say.

'What's that got to do with you?' a voice demanded from the doorway.

'Nothing,' Dalton said, turning to see Billy's associates enter the house. Dalton studiously avoided looking at their guns as they exchanged names. He learnt that the large man was Deke Grant, the other Paul Stark.

'Then don't go asking him questions,' Deke said, 'when he ain't got the strength to answer.'

Dalton smiled. 'Just trying to help, but I still reckon Jefferson will want to know how long ago this happened.'

'Time don't matter. We got him here as soon as we could. I'd have taken the leg off myself if I'd have known what–'

'The leg won't have to come off,' Billy screeched out. 'Will it? It won't, will it? Will it?'

Eliza hurried to his side and bade him to calm as Deke shrugged.

'Who cares?' he grunted.

'Deke!' Paul said, admonishing him with a shake of the head, to which Deke merely returned a bored grunt.

Billy began wailing and although Eliza stroked his forehead and murmured soothing words, it did him no good. Dalton started to pray that Jefferson would hurry up and put an end to this torment. He exchanged a glance with Paul who returned a wince, conveying that he also had the same concern as Dalton had.

For the next five minutes Billy continued to wail and Paul and Deke traded grunted comments. Eliza sang a lullaby, but this also failed to calm Billy, this young man now seemingly beyond all attempts to calm him, and so when Jefferson arrived, a crowded and boisterous room met him.

'Who are all these people?' he demanded as he barged past Paul.

Only Dalton paid him any attention and he started to introduce everyone, but Jefferson's exasperated glare made Dalton realize he didn't care who everyone was, just that there were too many people in here. The situation wasn't helped when Milo Milton squeezed in after him, ensuring that everyone had to jostle for position then stand shoulder to shoulder.

Jefferson repeated his question, his loud voice demanding an answer. This time everyone quietened.

'These men are Billy's friends,' Dalton said.

'Understood.' Jefferson pointed to the door. 'They will leave.'

Paul complained, demanding that he had a right to stay with Billy, but he soon desisted when Dalton started shooing everyone outside. He acknowledged Dalton with a short nod, then shuffled out followed by the stern-faced and grumbling Deke. Jefferson ignored them and, after a noticeable sneer of contempt at no one in particular, joined Eliza.

Dalton turned his attention to the remaining people. Eliza was kneeling beside Billy and would need to stay. Milo stood beside the door with his arms folded surveying the scene. Dalton raised an arm to usher him out, but Milo turned and set piercing blue eyes on him. Those eyes twinkled in the firelight and with him also providing a slight smile, Dalton decided he found something intriguing, or perhaps amusing about the situation.

'I have some knowledge of these matters,' Milo said with a brief and relaxed sigh. 'I'll stay.'

'And I haven't,' Dalton said. 'I'll go.'

Dalton turned to go, but Jefferson beckoned for him to stay.

'I need two strong men as soon as the water has boiled,' he commanded. 'You will stay.'

Dalton caught the implication and he lowered his head. Silence reigned for several seconds until Eliza spoke up and asked the question that didn't need asking.

'Why?' she asked.

Jefferson looked up at her with some compassion in his normally cold eyes then leaned over to look down into Billy's eyes.

'Your leg has to come off, lad. I'm–'

'No!' Billy cried out. 'No! No!'

Jefferson shrugged then stood back from him.

'If you insist. Where do you want to be buried?'

Eliza shot him a glance, imploring him to be more sensitive, but Jefferson merely returned that glance. Billy darted his gaze back and forth between Jefferson and Eliza then towards Dalton and Milo, his wide eyes begging for somebody to help him out of this nightmare.

'Maybe,' Dalton said, half-turning to the door, 'I should fetch one of your friends to be with you.'

'No!' Billy implored. 'Not them. Deke wanted to take my leg off before, but–'

'Then,' Jefferson said, 'Deke is a sensible man.'

'He isn't. I won't have it. I won't. I want my leg. I want my–'

'You've got no choice,' Jefferson commanded, speaking over Billy's continuing pleas. 'Your wound has mortified. Your leg is just a poisoned and dying thing attached to your body.'

Billy wailed then gave up on every last pretence of being brave about the situation. He flopped clown, threw an arm over his face, and cried uncontrollably with great racking gasps of total despair interspersed with barely audible pleas for someone to give him a way out.

'Let him have a few moments to think

about what you've said,' Eliza said, a calm no-nonsense attitude overcoming her tone and demeanour as she looked at Jefferson. 'Then we'll begin.'

Jefferson looked at the steam rising from the pot then shook his head.

'A few moments won't make this any easier,' he said. 'We begin now.'

Jefferson unfurled his rolled-up blanket to reveal a saw, this being one of the few pieces of equipment he'd brought with him. Billy raised his arm and clamped his tortured gaze on the saw, then screamed. He clawed his hands at the floor, trying to move himself away, but Jefferson ignored him as he hung the saw before the fire, ensuring the flames licked the metal.

Then he located a small bottle and a pad of cloth. He moved towards Billy, who watched him approach with wide-open scared eyes, shaking his head and trying to push himself away, but he was too weak to move himself. Everyone else watched, transfixed with a mixture of helpless concern and a desire for this torment for all of them to just end, each person's wide eyes clearly showing they hoped Jefferson could knock him out quickly.

'You want help?' Dalton said, asking more

to alleviate his own tension than because he thought Jefferson needed that help.

'No,' Jefferson murmured without looking up, but Billy had now summoned up enough strength to drag himself back a few inches and having gathered some momentum, he began to slide himself away.

Eliza clamped a hand on his shoulder and despite Jefferson's refusal of his offer of help, Dalton reckoned she wouldn't be able to stop Billy squirming away. He walked past Milo, but Milo raised an imperious hand, halting him.

'Wait!' he said simply, his tone still light and almost jovial.

'Why?' Dalton asked, glancing at him.

'I didn't mean you. I mean you, Jefferson.' He stepped forward as Jefferson looked up. 'I don't reckon it has to end this way. Perhaps we can save the leg.'

As Jefferson snorted, Billy stopped moving and transfixed Milo with his gaze, utter relief and hope etched into his tear-streaked face.

'Can you?' he murmured between snuffles, his voice just gulps of air.

Milo walked round to stand behind Eliza. He placed his hands on her shoulders and peered over her head at the leg then straightened up.

'I believe so.'

As Eliza shot a hopeful glance at Milo and even patted his hand, Billy sent up a howling hallelujah, but Jefferson shook his head.

'Milo, you are a resourceful man, but even you are no doctor.'

'And I believe,' Milo said, smiling, 'the same can be said of you.'

'I have never said otherwise,' Jefferson said, although the firm set of his jaw conveyed his irritation. 'But I have removed a limb before and saved a man. Have you ever saved a limb and a life?'

'I haven't.' Milo gave Eliza's shoulders a noticeable squeeze before he stood. Then he rubbed his chin, an amused gleam in his eyes. He didn't speak until all eyes in the room had been on him for several seconds. 'But I had a friend in Durando who once did it and he told me all about it.'

Dalton drew in his breath, thinking Milo had made a cruel joke out of this terrible situation, but Eliza nodded approvingly and Billy smiled hopefully for the first time.

'You had a friend...' Jefferson murmured, for once speaking what was on Dalton's mind.

'And he was a most intelligent man.'

'I cannot allow this to happen,' Jefferson blustered. 'You cannot risk this young man's life on something so ... so ridiculous.'

Milo raised then waggled a finger at Jefferson as if he was admonishing a child.

'But it isn't your decision to make. It's Billy's.'

Jefferson glared up at Milo as if he was about to deny this truth, or perhaps just snap him back for his impertinent manner, but then gave a reluctant nod.

'That is true, but do you really–?'

'Then we should ask Billy.' Milo knelt down beside Eliza. She started to move aside, but Milo bade her to stay and to continue to comfort Billy. She nodded, intrigue and hope in her fascinated gaze as she waited to see what Milo would do. She placed a hand on Billy's shoulder while Milo spoke with a soft and comforting voice. 'Billy, your leg is broken and the bone has split the skin. Poison has entered the wound. The broken leg won't kill you but the poison will. I propose to set your leg, then defeat the poison.'

'I just got one question,' Billy said. 'Can you save my leg?'

'My friend was a doctor, but I'm not, so you must make the decision. If I can't defeat the poison, the result will be, shall we say, most unfortunate. On the other hand, Jefferson wants to defeat the poison by removing your leg below the knee, but there's no proof that'll work. The poison could have spread and then he'll have to remove the rest of your leg and still it might not work and you'll die, slowly and in agony.'

'Then I choose your option.'

Jefferson grunted. 'That is just plain wrong. Stated like that anyone would choose to go with your plan. Most unfortunate ... slowly and in agony... You are misleading him. You are—'

'Be quiet!' Billy shouted, his desperation overcoming his youthful years and letting him command everyone's attention. 'This is my life you're arguing over. I'm the only one who matters and I know exactly what Milo is saying. He's giving me a choice between living as half a man or to risk dying as a whole man. I choose to remain whole.'

Jefferson glanced at his bottle then shrugged and placed it back in his blanket.

'Perhaps that decision is for the best. Now I can save my limited amount of medicine for more worthy people.'

Without further comment about the matter, but plenty of bad grace in his stooped shoulders and brisk actions, Jefferson gathered up his saw and placed it back in his blanket. He turned to go, but Milo bade him to stay.

'I need your help to set the leg,' he said, keeping his voice pleasant. 'And you might learn something you can use another day.'

Jefferson snorted his breath, his mouth opening as if he were about to snap back a riposte, but he settled for muttering a word under his breath. It was inaudible but Dalton saw his lips move and knew what he'd said.

'Southsiders.'

Milo didn't react other than to turn to Eliza.

'I hope you'll stay to assist me,' he said.

'It'll be a pleasure,' she breathed.

'It'll be hard work. Even after we've set the leg and we no longer need Jefferson, we'll have to sit with him night and day for several days to get him through the bad times to come.'

'I have cared for sick people before.'

Milo nodded then patted her shoulder.

'Can I help?' Dalton asked.

'No,' Milo said, his tone dismissive. Then he shuffled round to place his back to Dalton.

Eliza looked at Dalton for the briefest of

moments to smile before she turned back to consulting with Milo and Jefferson.

Dalton loitered for a while but nobody paid him any attention as they got to work. He watched Milo instruct Eliza in what she had to do, all the time holding her hands as he demonstrated her required actions in advance. Presently, Dalton accepted he had no reason to stay and turned to leave.

'Let's begin this,' Milo said, raising his voice. 'Together.'

'I'm ready,' Eliza said as Dalton threw open the door to face a sea of concerned faces.

'You are, but first,' Milo said, his voice soft and silky, 'let me hold your hands again. I want to check they're steady enough.'

Dalton couldn't help but stop in the doorway and look back. A twinge of jealousy hit him as he saw how close Milo and Eliza were sitting, and he thought about how close they would be for the next few days.

Then he chided himself for being so churlish when they were fighting to save a young man's life and he left. Outside, he urged the people who were milling around to leave, offered encouraging words to Paul, then headed back up the valley.

He had reached his house before the

weight in his pocket reminded him that he'd forgotten something. The crisis had stopped him asking Eliza about whether or not she'd like to own a gold trinket.

CHAPTER 3

'Whatever anyone else says,' Dalton grumbled, as he made ready to leave Loren's house, 'I just don't like that Milo Milton.'

'I thought it was those other newcomers you didn't like.'

'They don't bother me no more. They were just concerned for their friend, but as for Milo Milton – I don't trust him.'

'I believe you might have mentioned that before,' Loren said, smiling. 'But from what I've heard, he's been an asset to the out-siders since he arrived. Perhaps if he's annoyed Jefferson Parker now, he might stay with us and become an asset to the South-siders.'

'Perhaps, but there's one Southside he can stay well away from.'

'Then he's achieved one useful thing al-ready. He's made you think about how much you care for Eliza.' Loren chuckled and raised his eyebrows. 'And I've been thinking about how you could convert that gold nugget into a ring. I reckon it can be done.

So perhaps it might be the right time for you to give her something more pleasant to think about while she's looking after Billy.'

Dalton acknowledged the sense of this with a slow nod.

'I'll do that, but if Milo is still putting his hands all over her, I'll sure give him something less pleasant to think about first.'

Loren laughed, searching Dalton's eyes to see if he was joking, but having spoken his mind, Dalton turned on his heel and left. With Loren still chuckling supportively behind him, he headed down the valley.

When he arrived at Eliza's house, her brother Newell and Paul were sitting outside. The other newcomer Deke wasn't there.

'Is he all right?' Dalton asked.

'He has a raging fever,' Newell said, his tone somewhat bored as if he'd already answered this question several times this morning. 'But his condition isn't getting any worse.'

'Do you reckon it'd be all right if I looked in on him?'

'I'm sure it'd be all right for you to see *him*, for a short while.' Dalton smiled at Newell's emphasis then quietly slipped into the house.

Inside, Billy lay before the fire, sleeping. Blankets encased him from head to toe. His expression was peaceful, his skin was no longer clammy, and best of all the terrible smell of death that had enveloped him yesterday was no longer present.

Although Dalton had expected Eliza and Milo to be sitting close together, they were on opposite sides of the room. Eliza had tucked herself up in a blanket, her quiet breathing suggesting she was asleep. Milo sat with his back against the wall on the opposite side of the room, his legs drawn up as he looked at her with what to Dalton's eyes appeared to be the demeanour of a predatory vulture.

But when Milo looked at Dalton, he smiled pleasantly then put a finger to his lips and bade him to head outside. Dalton had hoped he might be able to talk to Eliza in private about his gold find, but he accepted he couldn't do that now. He also reckoned that the way things were going, he might not get round to telling her about it for days.

Milo stood and tip-toed across the room, making far too much of a show of being quiet with his exaggerated movements for Dalton's liking. Outside, he closed the door, again using exaggerated and slow movements to show he was being quiet then drew Dalton and the others away from the door before he spoke.

'My friend from Durando described the procedure to me well. Billy is making good progress.'

Paul nodded approvingly and, although he felt churlish in asking, Dalton couldn't resist putting an emphasis on his response.

'And how long will you and Eliza have to sit watch over him?'

If Milo caught the implication he didn't show it as he rocked his head from side to side.

'A few more days,' he said, then thought before he continued, 'maybe more than that.'

Dalton considered his response, wondering if it contained anything sinister, then shook off his concern and forced himself to smile.

'Please tell Eliza that I'm thinking about her and that I look forward to seeing her again.'

'I'll be sure to tell her that,' Milo said, his distracted tone suggesting he'd already forgotten the message.

'Is there anything I can do?'

'I doubt...' Milo paused then smiled. 'I'll need to continue sleeping here for a while, but I left my belongings with Jefferson Parker. Would you be so kind as to fetch them?'

'I'll do...' Dalton trailed off when Milo turned his back on him and headed back to the house. Dalton raised his voice. 'I'll do that with pleasure.'

Dalton watched Milo slip inside then looked at Paul and Newell in turn to see their reactions and to judge whether only he found Milo's behaviour odd and rude. Paul said nothing, clearly his concern for Billy blinding him to any other concerns, but Newell acknowledged Dalton's discomfort with a firm pat on the back.

'Don't you worry yourself about him,' he said. 'Milo may have saved Billy's leg, but that doesn't make him a man worth knowing – for anyone.'

Dalton provided a relieved sigh then turned to head over to the north side of the river, but his movement spurred Paul into reacting.

'I'll come with you,' he said, peeling away from the wall to join him. 'I ain't got much of anything to do sitting around here.'

They walked in comfortable silence until

they reached the river where Dalton directed Paul to follow him on the safest route across.

'You known your injured friend for long?' Dalton asked. He waited for an answer that didn't come, before continuing. 'You seem such a mismatched group.'

Paul shrugged. 'When there's not many people about you can't choose who you end up travelling with.'

'Perhaps, but you and Billy sound as if you're close, yet the same can't be said about Deke. He didn't even want to say how he got injured.'

'Discussing that won't heal Billy's leg,' Paul said with some finality.

As Dalton had once been a wanted man, he recognized the evasiveness that came with an unwillingness to talk about the past. But he had also vowed never to judge a man in the way he'd been judged before and he took Paul's comment in good spirits. He waited until they had passed the halfway point in the river then stopped.

'I guess when someone gets hurt in an accident, everyone ends up blaming themselves for the circumstances, and that just makes it plain hard to talk about it afterwards.'

'I guess,' Paul said with what Dalton took

46

to be relief that he had provided him with a ready explanation.

Dalton took a significant glance at Paul's gun.

'And I guess that a man who gets used to wearing a gun would find it hard to stop wearing one even when he doesn't need to. I know I did until I decided to stop here.'

'Don't know whether I'll stop here yet, but if I do, I sure won't see no reason to wear one.' Paul glanced back towards the settlement. 'That Milo seems to be a good man.'

Dalton noted Paul's unsubtle change of subject and he didn't reply immediately, wondering whether to confide in him in the way he'd confided in Loren earlier, but decided this man had enough to worry about.

'Don't know him, but I guess if I did know him I might say that.'

They set off across the second half of the river. Paul didn't reply while Dalton led him along the safest route, only speaking up as they waded out of the water.

'That mean you haven't been here for long either?'

'I've been here as long as most,' Dalton said, wringing water out of the legs of his pants. 'Milo only arrived a few days ago. I don't know whether he's stopping.'

'I thought in a small town everybody would know everyone else's business.'

'So did I, but it hasn't worked out like that.' Dalton looked along Two Forks' main road. Already several people were peering out of their windows at them. 'Everybody over here doesn't like us southsiders and for that matter, we aren't particularly taken with them.'

Paul followed Dalton's gaze then blew out his cheeks in exasperation when he saw the steady increase in the number of suspicious eyes watching them.

'You people have been right hospitable to us, but already I'm getting me the feeling these people ain't my sort of people.'

'Yeah,' Dalton said, pacing off down the road, 'but then again, I can understand their view.'

Dalton went on to elaborate on why many people here thought of them as a burden and how it had been only the early arrival of spring that had stopped that concern growing into outright hostility.

'I can see that,' Paul said. 'But you've got to welcome folk. It's only right.'

Dalton nodded, but it didn't change the fact that nobody here felt charitable towards a burden when they were struggling to survive themselves. It was no coincidence that the most self-sufficient southsider, Loren Steele – a man who never asked for help and who as a skilled hunter often had enough extra food and pelts for trading – was the only person the northsiders tolerated.

Milo's wagon was at the end of the town, standing outside Jefferson's house, and with Dalton's neck burning with the feeling that more and more people were watching him, he kept his gaze on that wagon. Without looking around or engaging in unnecessary discussion, they hitched up Milo's horse.

As Dalton had expected, their actions encouraged several people to emerge from their homes. These people watched them with their arms folded and disapproving expressions etched into their faces. Dalton acknowledged them with a friendly wave, then, to break the silence that was becoming oppressive, he shouted out to the nearest person that Milo had asked them to bring his wagon over.

Two people hurried off towards Wes Potter's barn without comment.

'Jefferson Parker won't like this,' the remaining man said simply.

Dalton wasn't sure of the speaker's name,

but he reiterated his comment that he was carrying out Milo's wishes. While he waited for a response that didn't come, Jefferson Parker emerged from the barn, the two people who had headed off to tell him the news at his side along with a trailing band of other men.

'What are you doing here?' he said, putting a considerable amount of contempt into his few words.

'Milo asked—'

'I know *what* you're doing. I just want to know why a southsider reckons he can walk into our town and take something.'

Dalton passed up the opportunity to provide a sharp reply and moved to climb up onto the wagon, but Paul spoke up.

'Milo needs his belongings and as he's saving my friend Billy's life, that's all that matters to me.'

Jefferson turned his cold gaze on Paul. 'You mean Milo needs his belongings to help another useless drifter.'

Paul snorted his breath then took a long pace forward to confront Jefferson.

'Let's go, Paul,' Dalton said. 'You're just wasting your time trying to reason with a northsider.'

Paul ignored him as he continued to glare

50

at Jefferson, and so Dalton placed a calming hand on his shoulder, urging him to turn away. Paul didn't move and with Paul's gaze boring into him, Jefferson spoke next.

'You two didn't listen to me. No southsider comes over here and takes anything from us ever again.' He pointed to the river. 'You can head back to your stinking hovels and wait. When I get the time to waste on you people again, I'll take the wagon over myself.'

'Like Paul said, Milo needs it now,' Dalton said, swinging round to stand shoulder to shoulder with Paul. 'So he gets it now.'

Jefferson provided a brief cold smile that suggested he'd been waiting for Dalton to talk back to him. He gave a small gesture with a finger.

Six of the onlookers stepped up to surround Dalton. Two men grabbed his arms. Two other men moved in to grab Paul. But they were too slow and Paul danced out of the way of their lunging grasps. Despite his initial success the other two men moved round to stand on either side of them, one blocking their way to the wagon, the other standing before Jefferson.

Dalton let the men get a firm grasp of his arms, feigning that he would acquiesce and

51

meekly let them turn him away from the wagon. But when the men relaxed their grips a mite, he dug in a heel and hurled out his arms, shrugging them off and sending them tumbling to the dirt. This only encouraged the others to move in purposefully.

Dalton lost sight of Paul amongst the milling people, but all around him fists rose and, although he didn't reckon there was any reason why this minor dispute should degenerate into a brawl, Dalton raised his own fists.

As one, the men around him rolled their shoulders, darting their gazes between each other to decide who should make the first move. The largest of them stepped forward first and drew back his fist.

Dalton didn't give him a chance to act and paced in, delivering a low punch to the man's belly that had him folding in pain and a sharp uppercut to his chin that cracked his head back. The man teetered back a few paces, but then gained his balance and to Dalton's amazement when he looked at him he was smiling, as if he'd let Dalton hit him to test his strength. And he'd found Dalton wanting.

With baying grunts of encouragement coming from everyone, he slowly moved in.

Dalton could hear scuffling feet behind him as Paul's own altercation developed, but he put that from his mind and concentrated on dealing with his first assailant.

This man spat on his fist and raised it, standing side on to Dalton as he moved around him. Then he took a long pace in. Dalton danced back a pace to avoid the punch, but it didn't come. Instead, his assailant's eyes opened wide and he stomped to a halt, his gaze darting past Dalton's shoulder.

Dalton didn't judge that he'd frightened him and he turned on his heel to look for the reason for the man's shock. He saw that Paul had more than taken care of the people who had moved in to deal with him.

Two men stood with their hands thrust high and a third was on his knees with Paul's gun barrel pressed right between his eyes. The kneeling man started shaking then pleaded for his life with barely audible words. When Paul spoke it was with assurance and with none of the lightness he'd used before.

'Milo Milton,' he said, staring over the man's shoulder to look at Jefferson, 'wants his wagon now and as he's looking after my friend, I intend to make sure he gets it. Is it worth getting this man blasted in two to stop me doing that?'

'There was no need to draw a gun to get your way,' Jefferson said.

'There wasn't, but the moment you tried to stop me, you gave me no choice. Now, do you understand just how determined I am that Billy gets the best possible care?'

'I do, southsider.'

Jefferson continued to stare at him, but as the man Paul was holding a gun on shot Jefferson a beseeching glance, he backed away a pace. In response, the men standing around Dalton lowered their fists.

After that, everybody backed away from escalating what could have been a disastrous confrontation. Dalton climbed up on to the wagon. Whereupon Paul pushed the man he was holding to the ground, stepped over him in a gesture of contempt, and joined Dalton. Although he still kept his gun drawn, he kept it lowered, then left it held across his lap in a visible but unthreatening manner as Dalton swung the wagon round then down the road to the river.

Everyone in town had seen the incident and, despite the gun, they all emerged to form a silent and disapproving line outside their houses as they watched them leave.

'Remind me,' Dalton said as they passed

the last house on the road, 'never to get in your way.'

'You couldn't, friend,' Paul said pleasantly.

'Where does a man go for entertainment in a dead-end town like this?' Deke Grant asked.

The other three men sitting outside Eliza's house all sighed. 'He doesn't,' Newell said.

'There's got to be something. You've got over fifty people living here.'

'Remember what I said,' Paul said. 'Those on the north side of the river don't mingle with these people.'

'I heard you, but it still don't answer my question – where do I go for entertainment?'

Everyone returned to watching the sun dip down towards the hills. After the altercation over Milo's wagon, Dalton had stayed in town in case there was more trouble. As it was, the afternoon had passed slowly with nobody venturing over the river to escalate the situation. Neither had any word come out from Eliza's house.

With Milo having said earlier that today was the key day when Billy would either fade or stabilize, Paul had spent his time walking back and forth. Even Deke, despite his surly demeanour and claimed lack of interest in Billy's health, had been agitated.

Newell gave a low snort, seemingly to nobody in particular.

'When we first arrived,' he said, his tone wistful, 'and the situation wasn't as bad as it is now, Wes Potter used to let us sit on the benches outside his barn and share a jug of his evil-smelling brew.'

Dalton laughed and rubbed his forehead as he remembered the pain that drinking Wes's brew had created the next morning, but this unpromising comment cheered Deke.

'Now,' he said, rubbing his hands, 'that sounds like entertainment.'

Deke turned to look across the river then got to his feet.

'Believe me,' Dalton said. 'It was never worth heading over there for.'

Deke glanced at Paul with his eyebrows raised, encouraging him to join him, but Paul provided a slow shake of the head. So when Deke set off, he wandered off to pace around the house aimlessly, kicking stones and grumbling about the lack of entertainment. Presently, Paul joined him and the two men mooched back and forth.

'You reckon the trouble across the river is

over?' Newell asked, watching the two men pace.

Dalton shrugged. 'For now, but Jefferson is getting easier to rile all the time.'

'I wasn't talking about Jefferson.' He looked purposefully at the two newcomers.

'Paul did what he thought was best to help his friend. Jefferson forcing a confrontation when one wasn't necessary concerns me more.'

'I can take care of Jefferson, but these gun-toting newcomers are a problem we don't need.'

'I had the same concern, but having spent time with Paul I don't judge him to be gun-toter.'

'And you say that after he held a gun to a man's head.' Newell sighed. 'And he's the calmer one of the two!'

'Wearing guns is the natural order of things for travellers around here – as it was for me once. If Billy lives, they could be here for a while so we'll have to learn to accept then and, if Jefferson can keep his temper, that'd help.'

'He won't need to. The moment Billy is fit enough to move on, they will leave. I won't risk annoying Jefferson again. We have a chance this year of putting the bad times behind us. Jefferson only distrusts us because we made life difficult for his people, but spring is here and soon we'll have crops growing and animals calving. Once the reason for last winter's friction goes, we'll start to trust each other.'

'It's a pleasant vision, but I reckon Jefferson enjoys being miserable.'

Dalton had meant his remark to be facetious, but Newell nodded as if he'd uttered a sage comment.

'I reckon so too. Jefferson consolidated his position as leader of Two Forks by unifying everyone against us. It isn't in his interests to lessen that friction, but most of the others will accept us when they see we're no longer a burden. And so I say again – the likes of these newcomers are a problem we don't need.'

Dalton didn't reply for a while, checking himself from making various comments. He watched Paul and Deke halt then look around, their arm gesturing showing they were having a heated debate, perhaps about whether or not Deke should go across the river.

'I guess,' Dalton said finally, 'even south-siders have their southsiders.'

'What you mean?'

'I mean Jefferson doesn't like us because we're newcomers, so you'd think we'd prove him wrong and be nice to newcomers ourselves. But here you are finding reasons to hate the next batch of people to arrive in Two Forks.'

'I don't hate them. I just want them to avoid making trouble then move on as quickly as possible.'

Dalton provided a low chuckle without humour.

'That's what Jefferson said about us.'

'He did, but we didn't want to move on...' Newell left the last of his observation unsaid.

Dalton searched for a way to disagree with Newell in a way that wouldn't annoy Eliza's brother, but he didn't get the chance to speak again as Eliza emerged from the building and beckoned them to approach.

Even before she spoke, Dalton saw the relief on her face and in the expectation of hearing good news he followed her inside. The situation was as he'd hoped. Billy was sitting up and leaning against the wall, spooning a weak broth into his mouth with his leg thrust straight out. He nodded towards them and smiled.

'I got me a whole leg,' he said simply, then

slurped another spoonful.

Milo stood over him, smiling in a fatherly way, then signified that none of them should come too close.

'I think we've beaten the poison,' he said.

'*You* have,' Eliza said. 'I just can't believe you did it.'

'Thank my friend from Durando's excellent advice.' Milo looked at Billy. 'And the strength and courage of this young man.'

Everyone stood, smiling and relaxing, until Dalton heard pounding footsteps outside. Paul hurried in.

'What...?' he blurted out. 'How...?'

'Relax,' Milo said. 'He'll be fine.'

Paul whooped with delight, stuck his head outside to shout out his pleasure to Deke, then hurried over to stand beside Billy.

'You got two legs,' he said, grinning and even jigging a few steps from side to side to emphasize his point.

'I sure have,' Billy said. Then the two men laughed long and hard, as if they'd been waiting for days to release their tension.

Eliza joined Dalton, smiling broadly, and Dalton rocked from foot to foot, uncomfortably searching for the right thing to say while not wanting to sound jealous after she'd spent so much time with Milo.

'There's one thing I've been meaning to ask,' he said. He took a deep breath. 'Have you ever wanted to own anything special, like a gold ... a gold trinket or ... or something...?' He shrugged as he ended his question weakly.

She looked at him with quizzical raised eyebrows, as if she'd expected him to say something else.

'I guess that'd be nice,' she said.

Dalton noted that Milo was looking at them, clearly listening in on their conversation and so he decided that he shouldn't say anything more just yet and instead enjoyed watching Billy's and Paul's delight. Presently, others congregated outside in the hope of coming in and seeing the miracle, so he slipped out to avoid the room becoming too crowded. Although the line of townsfolk was growing, all craning their necks to see ahead, Newell was making no move to go in, and he was scowling.

'Cheer up,' Dalton said, then drew Newell aside and lowered his voice. 'Billy is going to live and that means they'll be able to leave all the sooner.'

'Got nothing to be pleased about,' Newell said then pointed to the river. With Paul having gone into the house, Deke had decided on his own what he wanted to do next and was wading through the water, purposefully heading for the north side of town. 'When Deke heard the news, he decided to go in search of entertainment.'

'He should celebrate,' Dalton said cautiously, although he felt the same tremor of concern that Newell had so obviously felt.

'But not with the northsiders. I reckon if Paul is the calmer one of the group, then one night of that man's celebrating could ruin any chance we'll ever have of making our peace with Jefferson Parker.'

'Then come on,' Dalton said. 'We've got to stop that celebration before it gets started.'

They hurried after Deke, but even before they reached the river, Deke was wading out of the water. Then he started walking down the main road towards Wes Potter's barn. His pace was slow and heavy, and not at all like a man who was planning on having a celebration.

CHAPTER 4

By the time Dalton and Newell had reached the north side of the river, Deke was standing before Wes's barn. A row of men sat on the benches on either side of the barn door, enjoying their mugs of the infamous brew while looking westwards towards the setting sun.

Before them, Wes Potter had set out a rough-hewn plank over two barrels to serve as a counter. A barrel of his brew sat on one end beside several mugs.

The men slowly turned their steady gazes on to Deke, watching him set his feet wide as he stood before the counter. Across the river Paul had emerged from Newell's house and was hurrying after them, so Dalton and Newell slowed to let him catch them up. As they walked towards Deke, Dalton could hear Deke talking with Wes, his words harshly spoken.

'Give me a drink,' Deke demanded.

'I ain't serving no southsider,' Wes said.

'I got no idea what a southsider is, but if

it's someone who don't pay, then you ain't got a problem. I got money.'

This comment made Wes laugh and he considered the advancing Dalton and Newell before turning back to Deke.

'Your money ain't no use to us.' He pointed downriver then up into the mountains. 'The nearest places where anyone can spend money are White Falls and Durando. They're both two weeks away and nobody bothers heading there.'

'You don't use money?' Deke intoned, incredulous.

'Nope. We trade.' Wes flashed a wide smile. 'You got anything I want?'

Deke scratched his bald pate, his brow furrowed.

'I've only got money.'

Wes looked around to check he had his audience's attention, his smile suggesting he reckoned what he was about to say would be funny. This gave Paul enough time to hurry on to join Dalton and Newell.

Paul shot Dalton a glance, his raised eyebrows requesting an update on how bad the situation was. Dalton returned a sad shake of the head then whispered a suggestion that they should stay here until Deke gave them no choice but to intervene. So the three men stopped and stood in a group about ten yards behind Deke.

'I know something,' Wes said, 'that you can do that we all want.'

'Oh?' Deke said, leaning forward and stepping, perhaps knowingly, into Wes's trap.

'Yeah, you can leave town and take the other stinking southsiders with you. Now that's something we all want.'

Deke's eyes flared as Wes and the other men laughed loudly, throwing back their heads and roaring with delight with far more enthusiasm than Wes's weak insult warranted. Deke opened and closed his fists and, although Dalton didn't know him, he guessed this was enough of an insult for him to take out his annoyance on Wes.

'That ain't funny,' Deke grunted.

Everyone continued to laugh for longer than was necessary. Then in a coordinated act that added to the insult they all stopped laughing at the same time and joined Wes in glaring at Deke. Accordingly Paul took a single step forward and in acknowledgement of the danger of the escalating situation so did Dalton, and then Newell.

Seeing the potential for conflict approaching, several men rose up from the benches to join Wes, but then Jefferson Parker's authoritative voice ripped out as he walked around the side of the barn towards them.

'Take his money, Wes, and serve him,' he said. 'The southsiders aren't worth arguing with no more now that they've hired gun-toters. But just for this one drink. Then he leaves.'

Wes flinched, perhaps because he shared Dalton's bemusement as to why Jefferson had urged him to back down so quickly. The two men looked at each other until Wes gave a short nod. He tapped the barrel then filled a mug.

'One drink ain't enough,' Deke said.

Wes glanced at Jefferson, but Dalton spoke up.

'Believe me, Deke, one mug of Wes Potter's brew is enough for anyone.'

Wes and several men glared at Dalton, taking his comment as an insult, but, as Dalton hadn't meant it that way, he rubbed his forehead and groaned. This produced a genuine and rare laugh from several north-siders, which in Dalton's view relieved some of the tension. Deke also relaxed a mite then gestured to Dalton and the others.

'It ain't for me,' he said. 'One drink for each of my friends.'

Wes again glanced at Jefferson for confirmation that he should do this and again Jefferson nodded. Slowly, the milling men peeled away from the bar and returned to their benches, all murmuring their discontent that Jefferson had headed off what had seemed like a looming fight in which they heavily outnumbered the opposition.

Paul took his drink but as Dalton moved for his, Newell spoke up for the first time.

'Don't take it,' he said, taking Dalton's arm, his voice loud enough for Deke to hear, but if he had, he didn't react.

'Nothing wrong with taking a friendly drink,' Dalton said.

'There is,' Newell urged, attempting to pull Dalton away, but finding that he had dug in his heels, 'and you know you can't take this drink.'

By now, Deke was holding up a spare mug and Dalton realized he had to make a decision. Share a drink with a surly and argumentative man who was looking for a reason to start a fight with the northsiders, or side with Eliza's brother.

Dalton looked at Newell's hand until he raised it then moved in and took the drink. Newell muttered with irritation and turned his back on him while Deke beamed and beckoned Dalton in to join him. Dalton kept smiling as he cradled his mug against his chest then silently rejected Deke's offer and backed away to join Newell.

'Just take a drink,' he said from the corner of his mouth. 'It might stave off trouble.'

'After this afternoon, you reckon you're an expert in avoiding trouble, do you?'

'I know one thing for sure, this situation is mighty dangerous,' Dalton said, eyeing the northsiders who were still watching their every move with unconcealed contempt. 'Best thing to do is to keep things quiet, drink our drinks, then leave.'

'I'm not bothered about tonight,' Newell said. 'We have to live here after Deke's moved on and one drink could ruin everything with these people.'

'You're right. Deke could ruin everything, but look at it this way – this afternoon proved there isn't much of anything for him to ruin anyhow. Not taking a drink won't earn Jefferson's respect, but standing here and drinking a mug of Wes Potter's brew like everyone else might show we're no different to them and give us a chance of one day earning their respect.'

Newell furrowed his brow as if he hadn't considered the situation in those terms before then shook his head.

'We have different ideas about how to earn respect, Dalton. I have no idea which one of us is right, but I must do what I think is best.' Newell patted Dalton's shoulder and turned on his heel. 'Being here is inviting a repeat of this afternoon's trouble and I won't stay. You can, but just make sure there's no trouble, because if there is, it'll be your fault.'

With that pronouncement, Newell headed away. Dalton noted everyone watching Newell leave and as he saw many people glaring at his back with continued contempt, he took that as a sign that his own action was the right one – or at least was equally bad.

He joined Paul and Deke then looked around, searching for the man who Paul had pulled a gun on earlier. He noted him sitting on the edge of the bench and making an obvious display of not looking at them as he talked with Jefferson. For his part Paul also shot this man a few glances, but Dalton judged them to be more shame-faced ones than aggressive. He judged this as being another good sign.

For the next fifteen minutes they supped their drinks quietly, partially from having nothing to say and partially because the rot-gut Wes served tended to rob the drinker of the ability to speak.

Deke had no such problem and he downed his drink first then slammed his mug on the bar.

'Another,' he grunted.

Wes eyed the empty mug. 'The deal was you had one drink then left.'

'Yeah, but you like to trade and while I've been drinking, I've been thinking. I got something to trade.' Deke flexed his large arms. 'Tomorrow, I'm leaving town, but I'll only do that if I ain't got no reason to stay...'

Deke left the rest of his implied threat unsaid. Wes looked around but Jefferson had his back to him and was in animated conversation with the man sitting on the end of the bench, his foot raised to the bench as he leaned over him.

Wes turned back to consider Deke, his firm jaw suggesting he was weighing up the problems that'd occur if he refused to serve a large and aggressive man who wouldn't be around for long, then shrugged and poured him another. Deke grunted his pleasure at winning this minor battle then turned round to lean back against the bar.

'So you're moving on?' Paul said.

'We are,' Deke said. 'The kid's in good hands now.'

Paul sighed. 'I ain't sure I'm ready to move on just yet.'

'Then stay. I don't care.'

Deke made his pronouncement without malice then took Paul's and Dalton's mugs and paid for a refill. Again, Wes provided the drinks without comment and so they all leaned back against the bar and returned to being quiet, Paul and Dalton supping their drinks steadily and Deke gulping his.

Presently, as Dalton had hoped, the interest in their presence diminished. Jefferson kept his back turned to them and the other northsiders occasionally looked their way and laughed. But in a curious way Dalton reckoned his statement to Newell was turning out to have been correct. By standing here they were earning themselves an acceptance of a kind.

Despite his optimism, he still feared that a confrontation would develop and so he steeled himself when one of the men headed to the bar for another mug of brew.

'So,' he said, considering Dalton. 'Are you still a southsider or are you with these men now?'

Rarely had any northsider spoken to him when he didn't need to and Dalton considered this statement for hidden traps. As he found none, he answered honestly.

'I consider myself a Two Forks man. I live up the valley near to Loren Steele and like him I ask for nothing of nobody, but if I have anything spare, then I look to trade.'

The man opened his mouth, his sneer suggesting he'd had a retort in mind, but Dalton's reminder that he was a friend of Loren Steele had its desired effect and he sloped back to the bench with a full mug.

Afterwards, the laughter wasn't quite so persistent and Dalton noted that what could have been a disastrous night was in fact turning out to be beneficial. He decided he'd come down here again with Loren on another night and take a drink to let these people become more familiar with them and so consolidate their acceptance.

Later, while Dalton swilled round the dregs of his second mug, he exchanged glances with Paul, silently debating whether to leave now or have another drink, but then what he'd dreaded happening occurred.

The man who Paul had pulled a gun on this afternoon came to the counter. Wes identified this man as being Cox, and while Wes poured him a drink he looked at Paul with steady belligerence.

Paul tensed and his concern alerted Deke,

who placed his mug on the counter and considered Cox with lively interest. But when Cox spoke he used a civil tone.

'Is your friend with the broken leg recovering, then?' he asked.

'He is,' Paul said cautiously. 'The kid is a tough lad and he deserves the best.'

'Milo Milton is the best.'

'Yeah.' Paul sighed, perhaps gathering that Cox didn't appear to be looking for a confrontation. 'And about earlier... I wish there was some other way I could have helped him other than to pull a gun on you.'

Cox didn't reply immediately and in his furtive eyes Dalton reckoned he detected a mixture of emotions: respect, some fear, and plenty of relief.

'I guess if I were in the same position as you were, I might have done the same.' Despite Cox's level words he shot a harsh glance at Dalton, as if he was prepared to excuse Paul's actions, but not his.

'Then I hope there's no hard feelings.' Paul gestured at the mug. 'Be obliged if you'd let me pay for that drink.'

Cox nodded and took a sip of his brew.

'When will be you moving on?'

'As soon as Billy is well enough to travel.'

Cox continued to chatter in a way Dalton

had never heard a northsider do in his presence. This further encouraged him in his belief that the enmity between the two town groups would be temporary, but then Cox asked the question Dalton had hoped he wouldn't ask.

'How did Billy get injured?'

Paul didn't reply immediately and in the break in conversation, Dalton spoke up for the first time.

'Paul told me earlier,' he said, 'that it was a silly accident and he doesn't like to talk about it.'

Cox considered this information, nodding, and the matter might have ended there if he hadn't murmured a low, mildly interested comment.

'Oh?'

Dalton started to say something that'd change the subject, but Deke butted in with the inevitable response Dalton had dreaded.

'What's it to you how the kid got injured?'

'Nothing,' Cox said. 'I was just—'

'Then don't just go asking and get back to your bench.'

Deke waved an arm, pointing Cox's way back to the benches and although Dalton didn't reckon it was altogether deliberate, his inebriated lunge clipped Cox's mug and

74

sent it flying to the ground.

Cox looked at the mug, his breath snorting through his nostrils, his former pleasant mood evaporating with the same speed as the brew soaked into the ground. Then Cox raised his gaze to consider Deke. His fists bunched.

That was all the encouragement Deke needed. He slammed his own mug on the counter and squared up to Cox, but before he could escalate the confrontation Dalton barged in between them and faced up to Deke. He was pleased to see Paul also swirl round to face Deke.

'Move, Dalton,' Deke grunted, glaring over Dalton's shoulder at Cox.

'Can't do that,' Dalton said.

Deke licked his lips and rolled his massive shoulders, but Dalton didn't give him a chance to make his move and pinned him back against the counter. Paul darted in and grabbed an arm.

While the three men struggled for supremacy, Dalton heard the other customers leaving their benches and closing on them. Then Deke braced himself and with a grunt of triumph, hurled Paul and Dalton away. Both men fell backwards to land sprawling, leaving Deke to turn on his heel and confront Cox.

Dalton jumped to his feet, aiming to stop this fight before it got started, but before he could take a single step, several men surrounded him. One man wrapped an arm around his neck and held him from behind. He saw Paul receive the same treatment. He struggled but it was already too late as Deke fended off Cox's flailing blow then followed through with a brawling sweep of his large arm that hurled Cox to the ground.

A crash sounded as the remaining sitting people launched themselves off their bench with so much force they toppled it. Then everyone threw themselves into the fray. With all chance of diverting a fight having passed, Dalton flexed his arms then threw off the man holding him, but another leapt at him and bundled him to the ground.

Then that man hurled himself on top of him and the two men wrestled. All around him Dalton heard raised voices and scuffling sounds interspersed with the slap of fist on flesh. In a curious way, after this afternoon, this type of fighting didn't concern him and he hoped that even if he had to suffer a beating, neither Paul nor Deke would go for their guns.

For several minutes his hope proved

correct. He got into a two-on-one fight with two brawling men and in between trading punches he saw that Paul was also faring well in another two-on-one fight. Deke was taking on the rest single-handed, slapping aside everyone who came within range of his massive arms. Men went sprawling over the counter to roll towards the barn. Others went flying through the air before they ploughed into the ground. All the time, Deke laughed and even whistled, clearly enjoying having found some entertainment for the night.

But the noise attracted more people and with every newcomer siding against them, Dalton found himself facing several more people than he could hope to handle and he went down under the sheer weight of men. Lying flat on his back with two men pinning him down, Dalton squirmed but was unable to free himself. Steady kicks jabbed into his side. Dalton had a last glimpse of Paul getting the same treatment and even saw Deke going down.

Then a gunshot exploded, the sound muffled but followed by a screech.

The men who were pinning Dalton down froze and although he had a limited view of what was happening, the silence suggested everyone had stilled. Then a thud sounded, as of someone falling to the ground.

Dalton pushed his unprotesting assailants away and saw that his worst fears had been realized. Deke stood over Cox with his gun drawn and smoking, the shot man lying on his back with his chest holed and bloody.

To Dalton's side Paul had wrestled himself clear of his assailants. He was looking at Deke with horror, but he no longer had his gun, someone having made the sensible move of disarming him earlier in the brawl.

So the man who had taken Paul's gun found himself as the only other armed man here. He swirled the gun round to aim at Deke but before he completed his move, Deke turned at the hip and fired. His shot tore into the man's chest and hurled him backwards. The gun flew from the shot man's fingers when he hit the ground. A second shot ensured he wouldn't get up again.

Then the northsiders made the most sensible move in a situation where an armed killer is on the loose and everyone else is unarmed – they ran for their lives. Most ran into the barn, others heading around the side. Dalton, like Paul, didn't run, weighing up his chances of taking on Deke.

One look at the bloodlust burning in Deke's eyes as he took pot-shots at the fleeing men convinced him that all sense had fled from Deke's thoughts. Everyone was a target now.

Dalton ran for the barn. He was a few paces behind Paul as he concentrated on getting himself to safety before Deke's roving gun found him. He saw another man get a bullet in the back, the man running on for several paces before he stumbled and ploughed into the ground, face first.

Running as fast as he could, Dalton reached the safety of the side of the barn. He ventured a glance around the corner to see that Deke was standing with his legs placed firmly apart and was roaring with delight.

'Come out and fight, you mangy yellow-bellies!'

Deke fired through the open barn door then at the side of the barn, forcing Dalton to back away. He looked behind him. Paul and two other men were with him. Neither northsider spoke, but the contempt in their eyes as they looked at Dalton said all they needed to say.

Dalton turned away and looked towards the end of the counter, the only part of it visible to him, and he noticed the only way they could get out of this situation without further bloodshed. Paul's gun lay on the ground where the dead man had dropped it. The gun was about twenty yards away and about the same distance away from Deke.

Dalton didn't rate his chances of being able to reach it as high, but he reckoned he'd have to try. He steeled himself for making a run for it, but then Paul's hand clamped down on his shoulder.

'Wait,' he said.

'Situation ain't getting any better.' Dalton shrugged the hand off and darted forward, but only for a second as Deke tore a slug into the corner of the barn. He flinched back and gave Paul a rueful glance.

'Situation will get better in a moment,' Paul said. 'For those of us who can count to six.'

'What you–?'

Another gunshot sounded and at that moment Paul broke into a run, charging out from the side of the barn and running with his head down towards the counter. Dalton realized that Paul had been counting the number of times Deke had fired and so that meant he would now be reloading for the second time. He sprinted after him.

Paul was several paces ahead of him and Deke was punching in bullets while watching them run. Deke also backed away then broke into a run as Paul threw himself behind the counter to take cover. But Dalton ran past him and hurled himself at the gun. He rolled over it, gathering the weapon up in his hands, then kept the roll going until he landed flat on his belly, directed towards Deke and presenting as small a target as possible.

Paul jumped up and shouted out to Deke, perhaps doing the only thing he could do by presenting himself as a target and so in the confusion buying Dalton a few seconds. As it was, Deke followed Dalton's tumbling form and fired, his shot kicking dust a foot to Dalton's side. A second shot was just as far away, but by then Dalton had Deke in his sights and he fired. The shot was wild, but Deke flinched then thought better of staying to fight it out and turned on his heel.

Dalton loosed off several shots at his fleeing form, but all his shots were wild, as were Deke's returning shots over his shoulder on the run. When one of those shots cannoned into the counter, Paul dived for cover. A few moments later Dalton joined him in sitting back against a barrel, then he reloaded quickly.

Then together they bobbed up, but already Deke had reached the end of the road nearest the river. He was trotting along firing indiscriminately through windows and doors, taking any target, either real or imagined, and shouting out his contempt for everyone.

As he disappeared into the gloom, Dalton heard his last echoing cry.

'Damn northsiders!'

CHAPTER 5

Three men were dead. Four more had suffered bullet wounds. Although three of those were just nicks, the fourth was serious enough for Jefferson to send for Milo Milton to help remove the slug.

Although Dalton was pleased that Jefferson was putting the injured man's interests before his own disagreement with Milo, he didn't stay around to help with the aftermath, concentrating instead on finding Deke. Without any debate, he and Paul hurried down the road and across the river, following Deke's trail of destruction.

The moon lit their way and Dalton was pleased to discover that Deke hadn't carried on through the settlement on the south side. Instead, he'd collected his horse then took a route along the riverside, broadly heading up the valley and towards his house.

Dalton had left his gun there and so would have headed there first anyhow. Neither man spoke as they hurried up the slope, both knowing that capturing Deke was the only thing they could do to limit this disastrous situation.

They were within a hundred yards of his house when Dalton saw a figure ahead. It was stationary and was looking into the trees. Both men slowed as they approached, but, closer to, Dalton saw that the person was Loren. He hailed him with a wave and in return Loren gestured for them to keep coming.

'Over there,' he said, pointing, when they were close enough to hear him.

'Deke?' Dalton asked.

'Don't know who, but he headed to your house.'

Dalton quickly ran trough the details of what had happened. Loren remained stern-faced throughout and only when Dalton had finished did he sum up what everyone felt.

'Then we have to get him.'

They quickly agreed on a plan to surround the house and move in on Deke from different directions. As Paul was the only unarmed man, they agreed he should approach the house from the side while Dalton and Loren advanced from the front and back. Then they set off.

Dalton reached his position first and

shuffled down about thirty yards before the house, but, as he couldn't hear any noise emanating from the house, he decided not to wait for the others. He hurried on to his house then listened beside the door for movement inside before he backhanded it open. He still heard nothing from within and with him being sure that Deke had gone, he slipped inside.

Deke had strewn his belongings all over the floor, having clearly ransacked the house in a quick and desperate search for whatever he'd need to survive on his own. Dalton tensed when he heard footsteps outside, but then heard Loren call out.

'Has he gone?'

'Yeah,' Dalton said. 'Taking anything he could carry with him.'

Loren paced into the doorway. 'He won't escape us for long. We'd better get back to town and get together a posse.'

Dalton nodded, although he reckoned they wouldn't be welcome in that posse. He was about to follow Loren out, but then a worrying thought hit him. It surely couldn't have happened, he reckoned, but he decided to check anyhow.

He hurried through to his bedroom. It was a sparsely furnished room, but in the corner there was a rock which he'd painstakingly sculptured into a pillar, on top of which he kept his washbowl.

During Deke's whirlwind journey through his house, that rock had been toppled and lay on its side. Still, Dalton rolled the rock away to uncover the small hole he'd scraped away beneath and which was normally hidden under the pillar of rock. The hole was empty.

Deke had stolen his gold nugget.

First light was illuminating the eastern horizon when Dalton and Paul joined Loren in heading down into Two Forks. Last night nobody had been in the right frame of mind to begin the manhunt for Deke and so the decision had been made to pursue him using the better light of the morning.

Unfortunately a steady drizzle had persisted throughout the night and so when they'd searched around, they discovered it had covered up Deke's tracks and so made it harder for them to track him down.

Dalton called in on Eliza first, leaving the others outside. Milo watched them while she informed him that she had tried to help last night with the injured men.

Jefferson hadn't welcomed her offer of aid,

but there had been no more fatalities.

'Good,' Dalton said. 'And now I'm going after him.'

Milo smiled while she considered this information, registering her emotion with only a flicker of concern in her eyes.

'Then be careful,' she said. 'And tell Paul not to worry while you're gone. Billy is making fine progress.'

'I'll do that, but before I go...' Dalton glanced at Milo, hoping he might have the grace to leave them for a few moments, but Milo stomped his feet with an obvious motion of demonstrating he wouldn't leave.

Dalton wondered if he should still say something personal as he took his leave of her, but he merely smiled at her until she gripped his shoulders briefly then reached up to brush a quick kiss on his cheek. Then she turned away to fuss over Billy. He left the house. Milo followed him out and offered Dalton a huge smile.

'Like Eliza told you,' he said, 'don't you go worrying about anything, such as where the likes of you might get her a gold trinket, and especially not about her.'

'I wasn't concerned about her.'

Milo glanced into the house, possibly to check she wasn't able to hear him, but he still lowered his voice.

'I was only concerned that *you* might be worried. It'll still take at least another week before we can declare Billy as being well and we'll have to devote that time to being together day and night, day after day, being close together – looking after Billy, of course.'

Dalton had caught the implication in Milo's comment long before he finished talking and he didn't dignify it with a response. Milo then gave a low chuckle to himself and headed into the house, slamming the door behind him with greater force than he needed to.

While Dalton murmured unflattering comments to himself about the arrogant Milo, Newell arrived from across the river. His eyes were accusing as in low tones he reported that Jefferson's opinion of them hadn't softened since last night and the northsiders were viewing Deke's murderous actions as being their fault. In short, their help in tracking down Deke was unwelcome.

Dalton snorted. 'We're joining the hunt, no matter what Jefferson Parker says.'

'I think it's best to keep out of his way,' Newell said.

'Keeping out of trouble won't win no

favour with Jefferson or the other north-siders.'

'Perhaps not, but getting into trouble last night sure didn't help things and in the mood he's in, I judge that doing nothing will be the least worst option.'

'Your preferred option is always to do nothing,' Dalton said. 'But even if I failed last night, I reckon tracking Deke down now is the right thing to do.'

Loren and Paul grunted their agreement, but Newell shook his head.

'This is not open to debate,' he said, irritation burning from his eyes. 'We stay here and we keep out of Jefferson's way.'

Newell knew he didn't have the authority to order anyone to do anything and in other circumstances, Dalton would have been impressed that this normally docile man had gathered up sufficient conviction in his beliefs to issue that order. Newell cast a meaningful glance at his house, knowing that Dalton enjoyed his approval of him being sweet on Eliza, but also surely knowing this hold was insufficient to make him stay.

'Sorry, Newell,' he said, 'but I'm not listening to your orders. So unless you reckon you can stop us, either join us or be quiet.'

Newell was an ineffectual man but he didn't bear malice, so he provided a shamefaced shrug then shook his head. Other townsfolk had emerged from their houses to watch them talk, but none of them volunteered to go on a manhunt where they weren't welcome.

Dalton tried to put his irritation from his mind and along with Paul and Loren he rode off for the river. When they reached the north side they saw that Jefferson had gathered a dozen townsfolk around him and they were making ready to leave.

Just beyond the river and around thirty yards short of the group, they drew to a halt, but still the chatter amongst Jefferson's group petered out and most people looked at them with sustained hostility. Jefferson kept his back turned, perhaps pretending he didn't know they had arrived.

'Deke will head to the mountains and hole up there,' Jefferson said, gesticulating broadly eastwards.

Several men nodded, Loren included, but as Dalton was keen to prove they'd be useful, he spoke his mind.

'I don't agree,' he said then hurried his horse on to draw closer to the group. Paul and Loren paced on, but stayed behind him.

'I reckon Deke will head downriver to White Falls.'

'That's two weeks away,' Jefferson snorted, turning to heap scorn on Dalton. 'Only a fool would reckon he'd go there.'

'He wasn't happy with the lack of entertainment here last night and he spoke of seeking out more people. I reckon he'll head to a town. Durando is the nearest, but that's way up in the mountains and the terrain can be difficult at this time of year. White Falls is easier to get to.'

Behind him Paul grunted his agreement.

'I reckon you're wrong,' Jefferson said. 'After what he did last night, he'll lie low.'

Dalton saw that he would never convince Jefferson on this matter of opinion, especially as he wasn't prepared to divulge his reasoning behind his hunch. So he tried a different reasoning.

'That's what I, or for that matter any of us, might do if we were to find ourselves in the same situation, but none of us act or think like Deke does.'

Dalton reckoned this was a useful reminder that he wasn't to blame for what happened last night and he was pleased to hear several non-committal murmurs. They were far from support, but not the outright hostility Jefferson was championing. Paul added a supportive comment, but before the possibility of a change of opinion could gather momentum, Jefferson shook his head.

'This isn't a debate where we listen to the likes of you. We aren't heading downriver to White Falls. We'll search for his trail and track him down. You'll stay here.'

As Dalton had said everything he reckoned he could say, he looked at Loren, hoping he would take over and persuade Jefferson to back down. Everyone followed his gaze and slowly quietness descended as everyone awaited Loren's view.

'We'll be no trouble,' he said finally. 'And we do have valuable experience in tracking down men.'

Jefferson nodded. 'Then you can join us.'

'Obliged.'

Dalton hadn't expected such a quick climb down and all three men nudged their horses forward, but that only brought the response from Jefferson he perhaps should have realized would come.

'I said that Loren Steele is welcome. You two are not.'

'Hey,' Dalton said, but Loren shot him a glance, urging him to let him speak on his behalf, but, as it was, Jefferson then turned away and started issuing his final orders for the forthcoming pursuit.

Dalton didn't interrupt those orders and presently, Jefferson's group rode off along the side of the river, none of the men so much as looking at them as they rode past. Loren lingered behind.

'Follow on after us,' he said. 'And once Jefferson has calmed down I'll have another word with him and persuade him to let you join us.'

'And to persuade him to head to White Falls and not traipse around the mountains for days?'

Loren opened his mouth to speak, his eyes suggesting he was about to disagree with this plan, then closed it and headed off after Jefferson's group. Dalton waited for a while. Then with Paul at his side, they followed at a discreet distance of about a mile.

For the next two hours they headed down-river while Dalton waited for Loren to persuade Jefferson to let them join the group. He saw no sign of any change in the dynamics of the sprawled line of men ahead until Jefferson veered off from the river. The group bunched up and he saw a man who he reckoned was Loren close on the lead rider, Jefferson.

From such a distance he couldn't tell whether Loren was attempting to negotiate or, if he was, whether it went well, but the result was that a lone rider dropped back then waited for them. Presently, Dalton confirmed that it was Loren.

'Decision time,' Dalton said to Paul. 'Do you still reckon Deke will head to White Falls?'

'I don't know Deke all that well, but I'm sure he wouldn't hole up or head to Durando. White Falls is where I reckon he'd go.'

Dalton nodded, ready now to defend his decision. When Loren arrived he glanced back at Jefferson and his group, now heading to higher ground, then turned back and shrugged.

'Sorry,' he said. 'Jefferson would rather give up than have either of you go with him.'

'What about the others? I didn't detect that everyone agrees with him.'

'I don't reckon they do. Everyone saw that Deke was acting like a wild man last night and that you two did your best to stop him, but Jefferson is leading them and his view ain't going to change any time soon.'

'It'll have to when we bring Deke back.'

Loren provided a low snorting laugh. 'I

guess that's the only thing that'll help to heal the rift right now. I wish you luck with your hunch.'

Dalton hadn't considered that his friend wouldn't be coming with them and so he took a few moments to find his voice.

'You mean you're going with Jefferson?' he murmured, aghast.

'Despite all of Jefferson's faults he's keeping an open mind as to where Deke's gone. I agree with that policy – unless you've got a good reason for supposing Deke has headed to White Falls.'

Dalton sighed then nodded back towards Two Forks and gestured for Loren to ride on. They knew each other well enough for Loren not to question him and he hurried his horse on for twenty yards then stopped.

'Sorry about this, Paul,' Dalton said. 'What I'm about to say is for Loren's ears only.'

Paul's only reaction was a hurt look before he paced his horse off down the trail towards White Falls.

'What is it?' Loren asked when Dalton joined him.

'Deke stole my gold nugget. He must have happened across the place where I'd buried it last night. So he'll want to convert it into dollars quickly and White Falls is where the panners and prospectors from Durando head when they strike it lucky.'

'Sounds possible. But why are you so sure of your hunch that you're backing yourself to go on a two-week journey?'

'To get Deke,' Dalton said, shrugging.

Loren's gaze hardened. His jaw firmed, suggesting he wanted to say something but was forcing himself to keep quiet.

'I'm still going with Jefferson,' he said. He dragged on the reins, aiming to head on but Dalton stopped him with a raised hand.

'Loren, we've been friends for long enough that if there's something you want to tell me, you can just say it.'

Still, Loren didn't reply immediately and when he spoke his voice was low and reluctant.

'I don't believe you, Dalton, and I don't reckon you believe yourself either. You accepted that the nugget could change our lives for the worse, yet you're still deter- mined to get it back.'

Dalton shrugged. 'What with everything that's happened, I'd pretty much forgotten about the nugget. I guess I do hope I can get it back, but I want to get Deke more. And I don't want to then change my life with the gold. I'd just like a few dollars for when the bad times return and perhaps a precious trinket for Eliza. That doesn't make me bad, does it?'

'I can't answer that for you, Dalton. While you're chasing after phantoms down to White Falls, perhaps you might find the answer for yourself.'

With that statement, Loren rode away, speeding as he passed Paul, leaving Dalton to follow on down the trail with just one companion.

After Dalton had taken part in a private conversation that he didn't want Paul to hear, Paul descended into a sullen mood.

Throughout a long day's riding beside the river, neither man spoke to the other beyond the occasional comment about the route ahead. Dalton enjoyed quietness normally, but in this case it was an uncomfortable type of silence in which unwelcome doubts and concerns invaded his thoughts and stayed to haunt him.

He was worried about the deteriorating situation back in Two Forks. He was worried about his escalating arguments with Newell. He was worried about the stolen nugget affecting his friendship with Loren. He was worried about what Milo might be doing with Eliza while he was away, and most of all he was worried that all of those matters had affected his judgement.

Worse, they didn't pick up any hint of Deke's trail and he couldn't shake off the feeling that Loren was right and that this would be a wasted journey, and a long one.

After a night in which despite his tiredness Dalton didn't sleep well, the next day they set off at first light and, once they were riding, Dalton spoke for the first time in a while.

'You still reckon we're heading in the right direction?' he asked.

'Yup,' Paul said.

'Any reason why?'

'Reasons ain't changed since yesterday.'

'Anything you can tell me about Deke that'll help us when we catch up with him?'

'Nope.' Paul's jaw rippled, as if he was debating with himself as to whether to speak again and when he did, he spat out his words. 'And quit asking me about him. I know none of you trust us. I thought you were different, but...'

Dalton considered this information for a while, trying to create the impression he was unsure what Paul had meant.

'You talking about the private conversation I had with Loren yesterday?' He watched Paul nod. 'That was a personal matter between the two of us. We didn't discuss you.'

Paul didn't reply for a mile or so and when he did, his voice was less accusing.

'Maybe it wasn't.' Paul sighed. 'I guess what with all those northsiders whispering about me last night, I started to get guarded. But you just got to accept you can trust me.'

'I do,' Dalton said openly. 'But I still wish you trusted me enough to tell me everything you know about Deke.'

'And I wish you'd believe me when I say I've told you everything I can about him.'

Dalton didn't reply and with that matter sorted out as much as Paul was willing to, they did at least ride in a more companionable silence afterwards. For the rest of the day they shared thoughts about the trail downriver and exchanged infrequent but friendly bursts of chatter.

But they found no sign of Deke's passage that day, or the next.

During the third day Dalton began to seriously consider that this journey was a badly conceived one. By nightfall he was certain and as they started to look for somewhere to camp down he was ready to discuss when they should turn back.

Then they found the tracks.

A single rider had arced down from higher ground then ridden along beside the river. Both men smiled as they looked down at the tracks and those smiles grew when two miles on they found the burnt-out circle of a campfire.

They jumped down and fingered the cold ashes, both men agreeing this was the remnants of a fire from last night and so it was in the right time frame to be Deke's. Paul pottered around, staring intently at the earth at the signs of the man's passage and when he returned, he reported one fact.

'Deke,' he said.

'Don't suppose you'll tell me how you know?'

'Nope, but it's Deke all right, and he's just a day ahead of us. You reckon we can catch up with him before he reaches White Falls?'

'We might, we might not, but I'm just pleased we're going in the right direction.'

Paul agreed and they camped down for the night, this time in a more relaxed manner than previously. The sun had long gone down and both men were lying under their blankets when Paul spoke up. The fire was just glowing embers and not strong enough to light his face beneath his downturned hat.

'I've only known Deke and Billy for a few weeks,' he said, 'so I don't know enough about Deke to help us when we take him on.'

Dalton grunted then rolled over to lie on his back and considered how he could ask the questions that he'd like to ask now that Paul was willing to talk.

'I'm not prying,' he said finally, 'but how did you meet him?'

Paul provided a snorting grunt. 'Ain't much to say about how we came together. We just found each other, Billy broke his leg, and so we got him to help. We had no reason to stay together afterwards even if that shoot-out hadn't have happened.'

'Yet you're now helping me to find a man who you'd travelled with.'

'Even after Billy's all mended, I'd like to stay in Two Forks. I can't do that if I don't put right some of what Deke did wrong.'

'I can see that.' Dalton didn't press any further, but he still hoped Paul would add more. But several minutes passed without him saying anything and so he spoke up. 'If I tell you something, can I trust you to keep it to yourself?'

'Sure,' Paul said, his voice guarded.

'I decided to settle down in Two Forks because it was far away from most people.' Dalton rolled onto his side. 'I'd done some things in my past I wasn't proud of and there's always a chance that someone might come looking for me.'

Paul considered this information then rolled over to face Dalton, his face still in shadows despite a wind flaring the embers into low flames.

'I can well understand why a man might do that.'

'And so you can well understand why I might wonder if the same might apply to Deke, and to Billy ... and to you.'

'You can wonder, but I've got nothing to say.'

'You don't need to say nothing. Every glance, every gesture, everything you do all says that you're worried someone might come after you. I recognize the signs. I've done that myself, but I've learnt to live with it.' Dalton smiled. 'I mean, did you ever reckon I might have a past that worries me?'

'I didn't.'

'Then I'm acting in the right manner. You're not.'

Dalton rolled over on to his back to look at the stars and he would have been content to

102

let the matter end there, but finally Paul spoke up.

'Like you guessed, the three of us came together out of a mutual need to escape from some other people. We got away, but Billy broke his leg and so we got him to safety despite all of Deke's grumbling. Now, with Billy not going anywhere fast I'm worried he won't be able to defend himself if those people catch up with us. I intend to deal with Deke then return and stay with Billy.'

Dalton waited for more details, but when they didn't come he mentally added his own. The three of them were suspected of committing a serious crime. The people who were after them were lawmen. From the time Dalton had spent with them, he surmised that Deke was guilty and that the others were innocent.

On that basis, nothing had changed. He could still trust Paul, and they were closing on Deke.

With that thought, Dalton let himself drift off to enjoy a comfortable sleep for the first time in a while.

Deke was travelling quickly. No matter how hard they pushed their horses, they didn't close on him. After three days of early starts and late finishes they admitted defeat and set in for a steady journey to White Falls.

It proved to be an uneventful journey. So after twelve days of riding, they drew their horses to a halt on a mound and were able to look down on the town of White Falls. As they had maintained a gap on Deke of around a day, Dalton judged that their quarry would almost certainly still be in the town below.

'You got an idea as to where to start?' he asked.

'Nope. I guess we should just scout around.' Paul paused and when he spoke again his voice was gruff. 'We'll be more effective if we split up. You head into town. I'll search around the outskirts.'

Dalton noted the strangeness in Paul's tone and he deduced that this was because he'd rehearsed in his mind what he'd say beforehand. This meant the need to separate was important to him.

Dalton provided his own reason as to why this was – the lawmen who were after Paul could be here and he needed to avoid them. That meant Deke might also be acting cautiously and so a combination of Dalton's open searching and Paul's empathy with

Deke's situation should have the best chance of success.

They agreed to meet up at the mound at sundown. Then Dalton set off, leaving Paul to head around the outskirts of town.

On the way into town, Dalton put his mind to the problem of how he would find Deke. He started at the sheriff's office. A review of the wanted posters didn't reveal anyone with Deke's distinctive bald head and bear-like appearance. With the simplest solution proving unsuccessful, he decided to back his strongest hunch.

He asked around for details of the people who traded in gold, not the assayer's office, but the unofficial traders. He was directed to a mercantile and a beady-eyed weasel of a man who listened to Dalton's story with studied indifference.

'So,' he said with suspicion in his tone when Dalton had finished, 'you have gold to sell and so has your partner, but he headed here on his own.'

'We reckoned two men travelling separately would be the safest. The route down from Durando is mighty dangerous.'

The weasel didn't answer for a while and when he did, he didn't meet Dalton's gaze.

'Your *partner* hasn't seen me yet, but let's

not worry about him. Show me what you have to sell.'

Dalton caught the emphasis and knew that the weasel didn't believe his tale, but he also reckoned he was the kind of man who revelled in secrecy and so wouldn't see anything amiss in a rebuff.

'Only when my partner arrives.' Dalton paused as the weasel considered him. 'I have the bigger nugget, a real huge one, bigger even than a baby's finger, but we're partners and we share everything.'

Dalton reckoned the weasel would crack when he thought an even bigger nugget might be available, but he still denied having any knowledge of Dalton's partner, so Dalton decided Deke had really not met this man. He bade his goodbyes, promising to return when his partner arrived in town, and headed outside.

He took up residence leaning against a wall on the opposite side of the road to the mercantile where he could safely watch from the shadows.

The rest of the day passed quietly with no sign of Deke showing.

Dalton began to get itchy. He could wait for days and not see him, Deke could have ridden through town and kept going, or

106

there might be other unofficial gold buyers in town. Or maybe Deke hadn't even stolen his nugget.

He was just resolving to abandon his hunch and start asking around to see if anyone had seen a man matching Deke's description when he saw Paul for the first time since they'd parted. He was on the opposite side of the road, his furtive demeanour that of someone avoiding being seen. He sidled past the mercantile then set off down an alley.

Paul had said he wouldn't venture into town and presuming that he had news and had come in search of him, Dalton hurried across the road and followed him down the alley. He was just in time to see him slip out the back and turn to the left. Dalton hurried to the end and ventured a glance around the corner.

Paul was a dozen yards away, standing by a horse and facing another man. Paul had half-turned towards him and although the other man had his back to him, there was no mistaking his bald head and bulky appearance.

Paul was talking with Deke Grant.

CHAPTER 6

While Dalton watched Deke and Paul talk, suspicious thoughts tapped at his mind.

For the last two weeks he and Paul had enjoyed a companionable journey to White Falls and the mysterious past Paul had alluded to hadn't dampened that friendship. But he hadn't considered that Paul would side with Deke and he didn't like to consider that possibility now. So he watched them, giving Paul the benefit of the doubt and assuming he'd tracked Deke down and was laying the seeds of a trap so that they could get him later.

Accordingly, he viewed Deke's slap on the back and frequent laughing as a sign that Paul was lulling him into a false sense of security. When Paul pointed at a building further into town, Dalton viewed that as Paul planning to take him somewhere where they could easily overcome him later.

Presently, Paul and Deke set off along the back of the row of buildings. Dalton kept his gaze on them, but stayed in the alley until they were around two-hundred yards ahead.

He hurried forward, keeping his gaze on their backs and keeping close to the walls of each building he passed then darting into cover whenever he thought Deke might turn round. But both men paced along, gesticulating as if they were chatting amiably until they headed down an alley beside the building Paul had pointed to earlier.

Dalton then speeded up, reaching the alley a minute later. He glanced down the alley, seeing that both men weren't visible and that the building was a saloon. When he reached the main road he couldn't see either man and so he reckoned it was a safe deduction that they'd gone inside.

He looked through the window but failed to see either man, so he nudged through the batwings. The saloon was boisterous and teeming with hunters and prospectors vying for position before the bar, and Dalton still failed to see either Deke or Paul.

Casually he paced towards the bar, searching for a gap in the crowd as any man who'd come in for a drink would. He was several paces away from the bar when he heard Deke's strident voice cut through the general noise level. It came from further down the bar and as he was passing an unoccupied table, he darted down to sit at that table then drew his hat down. A few moments later he heard Deke again, his words unintelligible, but he was definitely standing amongst the crowd at the bar, around ten yards away.

Dalton saw Paul first, emerging from the block of men, closely followed by Deke then a saloon-girl. The group stood talking. None of them looked Dalton's way.

Paul and Deke were clutching glasses and the saloon-girl was flirting with them, resting a hand on each of their shoulders and smiling far too much. An obvious negotiation was taking place, the result of which came soon enough when the saloon-girl pointed to the stairs and sashayed off.

Deke downed his drink then thrust his empty glass into Paul's hand and headed off after her, licking his lips. Paul shouted a few words of encouragement to him then watched them leave. The moment Deke disappeared from view at the top of the stairs, he turned and headed for the door.

This is what Dalton had hoped Paul would do if his actions had been innocent, but he still kept his head down. As Paul passed he moved to place the glasses on the table, but Dalton thrust out a hand and grabbed Paul's jacket, halting him. He slowly looked up to face him.

'I can save you a journey, Paul,' he said.

Paul flinched, his free hand straying to his holster. Even when he saw Dalton's face, his mouth still fell open in shock.

'What are you doing here?' he gasped.

'Looking for Deke, like you.' Dalton gave Paul a chance to explain himself, but when several seconds had passed in which Paul's only reaction was to dart a glance at the stairs, Dalton's concerns returned.

Paul slowly regained his composure and sat opposite Dalton.

'And I've found him,' he reported.

'Good.' Dalton again gave Paul a chance to provide an explanation, something he felt sure he would do if his actions had been innocent, and again Paul didn't reply for longer than was strictly necessary.

'He went upstairs.'

'I saw. How did you track him down?'

'I backed a hunch.' Paul sighed. 'Are you going to get him now?'

'There's no hurry. Clearly you're sure he'll stay here until sundown, aren't you?' Dalton watched Paul furrow his brow. 'That was when we were due to meet up and you could tell me you'd lured him here.'

Paul winced then considered Dalton. 'You

111

don't trust me, do you?'

'Not enough to go up those stairs with you walking behind me.'

'Suppose I can't blame you for that.' Paul fingered Deke's empty glass before he spoke again. 'I won't lie to you. I didn't intend to tell you I'd met Deke. I'm treading a difficult path here and all I ask is that you understand that.'

'Then tell me the way it is and I might.'

'I'd probably be dead by now if it wasn't for Deke and no matter what he did back in Two Forks, I still owe him some loyalty. I didn't tell him about you, only that people were after him and that he needed to be careful, but he was already on the lookout so I wasn't telling him nothing new.'

'Obliged for the truth, but no matter how you explain it, Deke is your past and me and the rest of the people of Two Forks could have been your future. You had a choice to make. You made the wrong one.' Dalton moved to stand, but Paul raised a hand, signifying that he should wait.

'I knew that, but it wouldn't have changed what I did. Even if that's ruined our friendship, remember this – he only saved my life the once. My debt to him is repaid now.' Paul downed his drink and slammed the glass on the table. 'We'll find him in room seven.'

'I'll do the finding. I understand why you did it, but that doesn't mean I can trust you enough to let you come with me.'

Dalton turned on his heel and headed for the stairs. On the way up he glanced down at Paul and confirmed he wasn't following him, seeing him sitting with his head bowed, fingering his glass.

Then Dalton concentrated on the task ahead. Doors faced him on either side of the corridor. He paced along normally, not seeking to quieten his echoing footfalls, judging that being stealthy in a bustling saloon would draw attention to itself.

Room seven was the last one on the corridor, another corridor turning to the side after the door to run along the outside wall, which had a window through which Dalton could see down on to the main road. From within the room Dalton heard giggles emerging and the quick pattering of two pairs of feet. The sounds made Dalton imagine that Deke and the saloon-girl were chasing each other around the room in a playful act that was at odds with his perception of the man.

He could wait until the saloon-girl had distracted Deke more thoroughly, but he judged that waiting in the corridor increased the chances of someone seeing him then alerting Deke with a demand to know what he was doing. So he drew his gun, kicked open the door, and strode inside.

Deke had a long leg raised on to the bed, his large hands outstretched as if he'd been caught in the act of grabbing for the saloon-girl, who was at the foot of the bed. Dalton had aimed to dispose of Deke quickly and his roving gun centred on him, but the saloon-girl was between them and he didn't have a clear shot.

So he took another pace to the side, but then ducked away as the saloon-girl hurled an object at him. Dalton just had time to realize that it had only been a pillow, but it still folded itself around his face and he wasted several seconds prising it away. Then found himself facing up to the saloon-girl who clawed and scratched at him.

Over her shoulder he saw Deke bustling for the door, his gun drawn and only the presence of the woman standing between them stopping him from shooting as he himself had been saved earlier.

Then Deke hurried out into the corridor. Dalton saw him turn away from the stairs.

He batted the woman aside with more force than he'd intended, sending her flying onto the bed. Then he ran for the door, reaching it just seconds after Deke.

The corridor outside was deserted. The other corridor running beside the main road was just a few paces ahead and from down it Dalton heard rapid receding footfalls. He pressed himself to the wall then edged to the corner and listened, hearing a window open further down the corridor. He risked a glance and saw Deke slipping out of the opened window on to a balcony, a leg already placed outside before he steadied himself and fired at Dalton.

Dalton darted back, the slug burying itself in the wall opposite, then edged his gun around the corner and fired. Glass shattered, proving that he'd been fairly accurate but when he risked another glance he saw that Deke had now moved out on to the balcony.

He followed him keeping his back against the wall on the opposite side to the window and slowly the view outside opened up, and Deke wasn't visible. He could be waiting just below the sill for Dalton to appear and so he had no choice but to approach the window stealthily. He was two paces away when a gunshot sounded outside and a high slug flew through the broken window and hammered into the ceiling.

Dalton judged that Deke wouldn't have done that if he was still on the balcony and so he must have dropped down to the road. He bounded over to the window and looked down to see Deke making his way down the road, and he was hobbling. One glance at the twenty foot drop to the ground convinced Dalton that he'd probably injure himself too if he jumped down, so he darted back from the window then ran back to the stairs.

The gunfire had inevitably dragged many people out of their rooms, all in various states of undress, but Dalton's drawn gun told everyone all they needed to know about the situation. So, scurrying feet and slammed doors accompanied his dash down the corridor.

He avoided catching anyone's eye in the saloon while he bounded down the stairs three at a time, although he did notice that Paul had gone. He hurried through a parting gaggle of customers, all of whom were clearly skilled in the art of getting out of the way of a speeding armed man.

He dashed outside, turned left to follow

Deke but veered off to go down the alley and emerged at the back of the saloon. 300 yards ahead was Deke's horse, standing in the same position as he'd left it.

Dalton judged that Deke would head for it, but he would now be hobbling along the main road. So Dalton ran along behind the buildings, darting his gaze across the various small alleys and doors, expecting Deke to emerge from one of them. But he decided that Deke's hobbling was hampering him more than he'd expected because he closed on the horse without Deke appearing.

Twenty yards from the horse he slowed to a halt. He had passed several alleys, so he faced the buildings and backed away, letting him see as many potential places from which Deke could emerge as possible. No cover was available and so he had to trust his reactions were quick enough to see Deke first.

A minute passed then two and although Dalton reckoned he had the patience to wait for Deke to appear, he didn't judge Deke to be a patient man who would wait him out. So he could have abandoned his horse and headed in a different direction. He walked towards the nearest alley and glanced down it, but the alley was deserted.

He hurried down the alley to emerge onto the main road, but that was almost deserted, just a few people going about their business along with several people peering up at the broken window in the saloon. Dalton judged that this lack of interest wouldn't be taking place if Deke were still out on the road and so he turned and headed back down the alley.

He was ten paces down the alley when footsteps sounded behind him and he turned to see a man stepping into view. Dalton swung his gun round, but then checked himself when he saw that the man was Paul.

'Deke?' Dalton asked simply.

'I thought I saw him head down here – honestly.'

Although Dalton didn't trust Paul any more, he had to admit that if he had wanted to shoot him, he would have done it while his back had been turned. He offered a reconciliatory smile.

'You aiming to help me get him, then?'

'Can't say I'll help, but I won't hinder you.' He pointed. 'And I reckon he'll be heading for his horse.'

'Obliged,' Dalton said, although that aid was less than he'd hoped Paul would provide.

Dalton looked at Paul, giving him a chance to offer more. Then Paul's eyes opened wide, a warning emerging onto his lips, but before he'd managed to utter it, Dalton turned at the hip.

Deke stood at the end of the alley, his gun already in hand. Lead flew at him, the explosion of noise deafening in the confined space, and scythed into the wall beside his head then cannoned away. Dalton returned fire, his shot winging Deke's shoulder and spinning him away to land beyond the alley and out of his view.

Dalton broke into a run, reaching the end a few seconds later then slipped his gun round the side and fired. Deke returned fire, the shot wild and the report sounding some distance away and so Dalton risked heading out. He saw Deke hobbling sideways towards his horse, but on seeing Dalton he fired, the shot close enough for Dalton to reckon he felt it pass just inches from his cheek.

Dalton darted back into the alley. He looked over his shoulder to see that Paul was loitering at the end of the alley and showing no sign of providing him with more help. Then Dalton heard Deke's horse whinny, so he slipped out of the alley again.

Deke had mounted up. With the open countryside ahead he stood a good chance of reaching freedom, but Deke was the kind of man who only ran when he chose to and he never left behind problems he could clear up. He tore the reins to the side, turning his horse towards Dalton, then spurred it to a gallop, aiming to run him down.

Horse and man came bearing down on Dalton. Deke held the reins in his good hand, his injured shoulder causing his gun arm to waver in wild circles. A slug blasted into the ground beside him, but Dalton kept his footing and faced the advancing rider. He steadied his aim then took his best shot. Deke was just yards from him as he fired and immediately afterwards, Dalton threw himself to the side, rolled, and slammed to a halt pressed against the wall.

A huge thud sounded behind him and when he rolled to his knees, he saw Deke rolling across the ground clutching his chest. He twitched, levered himself up on his good arm and swung round to face Dalton. But even as Dalton was turning his gun on him, Deke arched his back, a pained grunt tore from his lips, and he flopped down to bury his face in the dirt.

Dalton still approached him cautiously,

120

but when he kicked him over, Deke rolled onto his back, his chest red and stilled.

Although the nugget hadn't been the most important thing on Dalton's mind, he hunkered down beside him and frisked him, but Deke didn't have the nugget on him, and neither did he have enough money to suggest he'd sold it.

A check of Deke's saddle-bag revealed the same result. Deke didn't have the nugget. He couldn't have been the one who stole it.

Dalton was still trying to assimilate this information when from the corner of his eye he noticed that someone was watching him. He looked up, expecting to see Paul, but faced a new man, who stood beside the alley considering him with a cold accusatory glare. His hand rested on his gunbelt with the easy nature of a man who reckoned he could draw quickly. Dalton looked around but saw no sign of Paul, or anyone else.

'Step away from that man,' the newcomer said.

'I'll do that, but before you get yourself involved you need to know I had no choice but to kill this man. He was a killer and I've been tracking him for some time. My name is Dalton. His name was Deke Grant.'

On hearing Deke's name the man's eyes

flared with recognition.

'Then you've done this town and me a great service, Dalton.'

'Obliged for that...' Dalton raised his eyebrows.

The man smiled then parted his jacket for Dalton to see his star.

'I'm the sheriff of White Falls,' he said. 'Sheriff Rory Blake.'

CHAPTER 7

'Sounds like you and the good citizens of Two Forks had a rough time at the hands of Deke Grant,' Sheriff Rory Blake said as he handed Dalton another cup of coffee.

Dalton nodded and sipped the coffee. For the last hour he had sat in the law office while Rory probed him about the events that had taken place in White Falls and before in Two Forks. Rory had accepted Dalton's need to kill Deke, but he had pried for more details. Although Dalton had related a true version of events, in that what he'd said was true, he'd failed to reveal all the details.

After Paul had double-crossed him by meeting Deke, Dalton owed him no favours, but Paul had inadvertently led him to Deke and he had warned him of his presence in the alley. Also Billy had seemed a pleasant enough young man and so deserving of a second chance.

'Deke was a mean one and that's the truth,' Dalton said, finishing off his tale.

'See anyone with him?' Rory asked.

Dalton raised his eyebrows, conveying that this question had surprised him and he hadn't considered that Deke might have accomplices.

'Nope, but then again Two Forks is a long way from anyone. We don't get many visitors.'

Dalton hoped his emphasis on how far away Two Forks was from White Falls would ensure Rory would never embark on such a journey to check out his version of events, and sure enough, Rory nodded.

'Never been there myself. Don't reckon I ever will, no matter how fine a place it sounds.'

Dalton avoided sighing with relief, but reckoned it was natural for him to ask a follow-up question.

'Do you mean there are others like him out there? I'd hate to think another Deke Grant might ride into town and raise hell.'

'He had two accomplices, Paul Stark and Billy Boyd. Neither were as ornery as he was, but I'd still keep on the lookout for them.'

Dalton agreed that he would and when he'd finished his coffee, he decided that the longer he stayed here, the greater the chance he would accidentally reveal something that would cause Paul a problem. He pointed to the door.

'Can I go now?'

'In a moment,' Rory said, and headed to his desk. He rummaged inside and returned clutching the largest wad of dollars Dalton had ever seen.

'I don't need no reward for getting the man who shot up our town.'

'I know, but there was already a five-hundred dollar reward on Deke Grant's head.' Rory began counting the bills into Dalton's hand.

'Even though there wasn't a wanted poster outside.'

'There's one up in Durando.' Rory paused from counting. 'Deke and his accomplices robbed and killed a man up there, a doctor by the name of Zachary Jones, a good man and worth ten of each one of them.'

'Obliged for the information. It makes me feel easier about taking the money.'

Rory restarted his counting. 'Good. It's worth each and every dollar to be rid of him. And if you ever meet the other two, information on them will be worth the same again.'

Rory placed the last bill in Dalton's hand then met Dalton's gaze.

'I'll be sure to remember that,' Dalton said evenly, closing his grasp around the money.

On the day after he'd caught up with Deke, Dalton led his newly acquired second horse into the hills as he embarked on the long journey back to Two Forks. He hadn't seen Paul again since he'd disappeared, presumably because he was avoiding Sheriff Blake.

Dalton still had $200 of his reward money left, but he'd converted the rest into the kind of items he would have bought if he'd been able to reclaim his gold nugget. As he'd earned those items through his own efforts, he allowed himself to enjoy a certain smug feeling.

So now he had plenty of items to trade when he arrived back in Two Forks, including the kind of metalwork that nobody could make and foodstuffs nobody could grow. He had also bought medical supplies and several frivolous items, including a present for Eliza.

To ensure he reached town on his own with his purchases intact, he'd invested in a rifle.

As it was, he rode on throughout the day without seeing anyone and if the journey back proved to be as uneventful as the journey to White Falls had been, he wouldn't complain.

That night, Dalton cooked up a mess of beans and beef on his new pan then settled down beneath his new blanket, looking up at the stars. He'd been pondering on what might be happening back at Two Forks for an hour when he heard a twig snap nearby. With him being alone and loaded down with plenty of valuable acquisitions, he was already alert to the possibility of receiving unwelcome visitors, but he also hoped he knew who this particular visitor was.

He still edged his gun up to his chest under his blanket while continuing to present the profile of a dozing man. Then he again heard a twig snap and he accepted that this visitor wasn't trying to approach him stealthily.

'Howdy, Paul,' he said.

He heard a sharp intake of breath from the darkness of the bushes. Then Paul spoke.

'I ain't here to cause you no trouble, Dalton,' he said.

'Then come out into the light and I'll believe you.'

Paul stepped into the arc of firelight, holding his hands high.

'I just thought I ought to see you and give

you an explanation.'

'Don't need one of those, so you can leave with your mind at rest, and you can relax about Sheriff Blake too. I didn't tell him nothing about you.'

'Obliged,' Paul said with a sigh of relief. He requested Dalton's permission to move using a quick nod then hunkered down by the campfire and warmed his hands. 'You didn't have to do that.'

'I didn't.'

'But know this – I'd never have sided with Deke against you, but neither could I side with you against him.'

'I saw that, but like I said, I don't need no explanation from you.' Dalton kept his voice cold, not inviting Paul to continue with his excuses and so letting him leave when he chose to without rancour, but Paul paced round the campfire to stand closer to him.

'You do when I want to return to Two Forks.'

Dalton gave a slow shake of his head. 'I accept your reasoning for what you did in White Falls and in the same circumstances I might have done the same myself, but that doesn't mean I can trust you no more. You're free to do whatever you want to do, but you're not travelling with me.'

'I understand, but it'd be safer for both of us if we travelled together.'

'I've got stuff worth stealing now. You haven't. I reckon you'd be safer on your own.'

'I reckon I would, but I'm prepared to help you now that you've disposed of Deke.' Paul looked at Dalton, but Dalton merely returned his gaze. Paul sighed. 'Then before you turn me away, you'd better hear my full story. Deke, Billy and me were Sheriff Rory Blake's prisoners. We escaped.'

'I worked most of that out some time ago, but what worries me more is that you only chose to tell me that after I'd met Sheriff Blake and learnt all about you.'

'I guess when you're a wanted man everything you do looks bad.'

'I guess it does,' Dalton said, feeling the first glimmer of sympathy for Paul in a while. He understood how a man who was wanted for a crime could easily have his every action questioned. 'I suppose you're now going to tell me you're all innocent.'

'I am and I'm sure Billy is. And Deke was the kind of man who boasted about the things he'd done. He'd have told me if he'd done whatever Sheriff Blake reckoned we'd done.'

'Which was?'

'I don't know.' Paul shrugged and spread his hands, but when Dalton snorted his disbelief, he raised his voice. 'I don't know, honestly.'

'Then don't tell me what you didn't do. Tell me what you did.'

Paul took a deep breath before he responded and when he spoke his voice was low and to Dalton's ears, his tone was honest.

'We were three men who'd stopped over in Durando with toothache—'

'Toothache!'

'Yeah. Billy went in first to see this man who could pull teeth. He gave him something to knock him out. I requested the same treatment but just as I was passing out, Deke came in demanding to be treated next. That was it. When I came to, I was in a mobile cell with Deke and Billy heading off to White Falls. None of us knew why we were being held and Rory Blake wouldn't tell us nothing.'

Dalton considered this information and although he had no reason not to believe it, it didn't change the fact that Paul was a wanted man who had double-crossed him.

'I sympathize, and having heard that, I

repeat that you and I can walk away from each other without me harbouring a grudge.'

'Glad to hear it, but are you saying I can't go back to Two Forks?'

'I am. You'll have to find somewhere else to make a fresh start.' Dalton considered what he'd said and as he reckoned it had been unnecessarily harsh, he continued. 'I told the sheriff that Deke rode into Two Forks on his own and I can't risk him ever checking out my story. I'll advise Billy to move on as soon as he can and I'll try to persuade everyone to forget you were ever in town.'

For long moments Paul looked at Dalton, but Dalton kept his gaze firm, confirming he wouldn't change his mind, and slowly Paul nodded.

'I guess,' he said, his tone hurt but resigned, 'that was the best I could have hoped for. But before I go, one other matter – did Sheriff Blake mention what we were supposed to have done?'

Dalton had deliberately not mentioned this and he reckoned only an innocent man would ask this as his final question. It didn't change his view on Paul. This man had run out on him when he'd faced a life or death struggle with Deke Grant and that was something he couldn't forgive.

'You killed a man called Doctor Zachary Jones in Durando, your dentist apparently.'

'That sure is news to me,' Paul said with some relief in his tone. He tipped his hat. 'But knowing what I'm wanted for might help me one day.'

Slowly, Paul paced back into the bushes. Dalton heard twigs snap as he took his leave of him. Then there was silence.

The encounter left Dalton feeling restless. He'd vowed never to judge a man in the way he'd been judged in the past. Although Paul's actions during his confrontation with Deke warranted the tough line he'd taken, it didn't stop him from having a sour taste in his mouth.

So he lay for another hour brooding with sleep refusing to come and was therefore wide awake when he again heard a twig snap nearby. He started to tell Paul to go away, but the words died on his lips when he heard a second sound, a rustling, also coming from ahead but several yards to the right of the first noise.

Two people were heading towards his campfire and these people were probably not trying to be stealthy either. Dalton kept his gun held low and ready, aiming through the blanket at the approaching people. Sure enough, first one form then a second emerged from the darkness.

'That's far enough,' Dalton said. He watched the two men come to an abrupt halt. 'Then put those hands where I can see them and step closer to the light.'

'We ain't trouble,' the man on the right said, his colleague echoing his comment. Both men were rough-clad, garbed as hunters with hide coats, so they could have a legitimate reason for seeking out the warmth of his campfire.

'Then what are you doing sneaking around in the dead of night?'

'We weren't doing no sneaking.' The man's voice was loud and possibly offended by Dalton's comment. 'We just wanted to share your heat for the night.'

'Then you should have made yourself known earlier and asked to be invited in.'

'Thought we were doing that. We weren't exactly being quiet.'

'I guess you weren't.' Dalton gestured towards the other side of the campfire, the motion freeing his blanket and letting them see he'd levelled a gun on them.

The talkative man flinched, his darting and wide eyes again seeming offended by

Dalton's disbelief, but the silent man just shrugged. His gaze drifted towards Dalton's laden horse and lingered there. He licked his lips.

A tremor of worry surged through Dalton's innards a moment before he heard a crisp footfall sound behind him. Only his heightened senses made him alert enough to sit up straight, turn, and sight the bearded man with a drawn gun who was sneaking up on him. But he didn't fire.

The bearded man wasn't the only one closing on him. Three men were pacing into the firelight in a line, each several yards apart, and all with guns drawn and aimed down at him.

Dalton acknowledged with a rueful snort that the first two men hadn't disguised their arrival so that they could distract him from noticing the three men who *were* being stealthy.

'Now,' the talkative man said from behind him, 'it's time we found out what you've been buying.'

Dalton reckoned there was nothing he could say or do to stop these men from taking everything he'd bought. He still kept his gun on the bearded man while he consoled himself with the thought that he'd ridden into White Falls with nothing. As long as he could get out this situation alive, he'd lost nothing. But that hope evaporated when the silent man spoke for the first time.

'I reckon,' he said, 'whoever kills him gets his horses.'

'That ain't a fair deal,' the bearded man said. 'He's aiming at me.'

'That ain't my problem.'

The bearded man darted his gaze up to chide the quiet man, the others looking at them as they enjoyed the potential brewing argument.

Dalton reckoned this distraction would be the best chance he'd get. He fired, slamming the bearded man on to his back, then rolled himself away from the campfire, aiming to reach the only cover available of the shadows. Bullets kicked dirt behind his tumbling form as, after two rolls, he thrust himself forward and gained his feet, coming up bent double and running forward.

Then he immediately threw himself to the side, hearing the whine of bullets as the raiders tried to follow him with wild splaying gunfire. He hit the ground, rolled once and landed on his belly looking straight back towards the campfire.

All four remaining men had swung round

to face him. With the safety of the shadows some ten yards away Dalton didn't reckon he'd either have enough time to get to safety or take out all four men.

But he tried, shooting one of the middle men, his shot winging his arm and sending him flying back into the campfire.

This lucky break, for Dalton, resulted in the man screeching in pain and rolling away, his coat sleeves ablaze. One of the other men moved to help him and Dalton made him pay for his kind act by blasting him through the side.

The other two men ignored the burning man and aimed down at him with calm assurance. Dalton started to swing his gun towards them, but long before he could aim at them a gunshot rang out, then a second.

But none of the shots had been aimed at Dalton and he saw first one man then the other stumble to his knees, then keel over face first into the dirt, a large smoking hole in each of their backs.

Only when another shot rang out and the burning man stopped his frantic twitching did Dalton accept what had happened. He stood and welcomed the form that was loitering on the edge of the clearing.

'Mighty pleased to see you, Paul,' he said.

'I owed you that before I left.' Paul turned to leave.

'You did,' Dalton shouted, his raised voice halting his saviour. 'But now I owe you. You may have saved Deke Grant's life the once, but you just saved my life at least twice.' Dalton gestured at the campfire. 'Perhaps you'd like to enjoy the warmth tonight.'

Paul provided a slow nod and turned round to face the campfire.

'I would,' he said evenly.

'And then tomorrow, we'll have to rise early.' Dalton offered a smile as he pointed westwards. 'We've got a long journey ahead of us back to Two Forks.'

'Obliged for the offer, but I've been thinking. I don't want to go back to Two Forks just yet. I can't run from the law all my life because of a crime I didn't commit. I intend to find the man who really killed Zachary Jones and clear my name.'

'Then you made the right choice this time, but you're wrong about one thing.' Dalton smiled. '*We* will find the man who really killed Zachary Jones and clear your name.'

CHAPTER 8

Dalton lingered his gaze on the town ahead. After a month away, Two Forks had never looked so welcoming.

They had made good time on the return journey and had not encountered any further problems after seeing off the bushwhackers. Although Paul had initially not wanted to come here, they'd ultimately decided to return to Two Forks before embarking on the journey to Durando, the only place where they might uncover the truth about Zachary Jones's murder.

They hadn't come up with any ideas about how they'd achieve that, but for now, Dalton was letting his thoughts dwell on his homecoming.

Despite a lot of brooding over the last few days, he was unsure whether he should be more worried about Milo having had the time to get closer to Eliza, whether Jefferson's attitude to the southsiders had worsened, or whether he would be able to resolve his arguments with Newell and Loren.

As it was he quickly got an inkling of the state of all four problems. Most of the southsiders were working in the fields and Newell saw and hailed them first. He led a straggling, but smiling band of townsfolk down to the trail to meet them.

When Dalton saw Billy hobbling across the fields towards them, he decided that he had become an accepted part of the community, suggesting that nobody bore the newcomers any ill-will because of Deke's activities. He exchanged pleasantries with Newell without friction while the other townsfolk milled around. Everyone hooted in pleasure when they heard about Deke Grant's demise.

'Where's Eliza?' Dalton asked Newell as soon as he got the chance.

Newell glanced away before he answered.

'Not too sure. I think she's with Milo.' Newell shuffled from foot to foot. 'She's been doing that a lot since Billy was well enough to walk unaided.'

Dalton nodded, accepting that Newell was hinting at plenty of problems with that simple comment. He also asked about Loren, but Newell hadn't seen him much recently. Jefferson's group had returned after a week of searching for Deke, and Loren had reported that they'd picked up no trace of him. None of the northsiders had talked to them about their experiences, or about anything else for that matter.

Newell viewed this lack of contact as a good thing.

When Billy arrived, Paul was pleased to see how well he'd mended and as they set about chatting amiably, Dalton decided he should go on his own to see Jefferson and report on his success. He didn't mention this to Newell, heading broadly towards his house before veering off to the river when he was well away from the group in the fields.

This wasn't something he wanted to do, but he reckoned he had to. He'd already thought through what he'd say to Jefferson to avoid him sounding as if he was gloating at his success, but he still didn't expect the meeting to go well. He wasn't disappointed.

Even while he was fording the river, a delegation of northsiders emerged from deeper in the town to stand before their houses. Jefferson stood at the front with a solid wall of people standing behind him. With pitchforks and even a few guns displayed, everyone looked as if they were preparing to defend the town against an onslaught of marauding bandits.

Dalton dismounted and led both horses towards them, keeping his expression pleasant. Jefferson and the others scowled.

'That's close enough, Dalton,' Jefferson said. 'No southsider steps foot in our town again.'

'Two Forks is all one town,' Dalton said, then raised his voice as Jefferson barked out a denial. 'But that's not what I've come to tell you. We dealt with Deke Grant.'

Jefferson's scowl stayed although his briefly raised eyebrows registered some relief.

'Dealt?'

'We finally caught up with him in White Falls. I tried to take him peaceably so that I could hand him over to Sheriff Blake who could ensure he'd receive proper justice in a court of law, but he gave me no choice but to shoot and kill him.'

Several people grunted their approval, but Jefferson sneered. 'And your version of justice is supposed to be a comfort to the families of the people he killed, is it?'

Dalton forced himself not to smile. Jefferson had headed off on a mission to find Deke and he'd have had no qualms about killing him, yet he was taking a contrary view just to browbeat him some more. Several people glanced at Jefferson as if they didn't agree with what he'd said before they returned to glaring at him.

'I never said it should,' Dalton said, forcing himself to keep his tone light and friendly. 'We just tracked him down and did what we had to do.'

Jefferson looked over Dalton's shoulder and narrowed his eyes as he peered across the river.

'And I suppose that means Paul has returned with you to join Deke's other useless friend?'

'I would never have found Deke if it hadn't have been for Paul,' Dalton said, stretching the truth to breaking point. 'You should appreciate that. And you should also accept that neither of them are like Deke.'

'I'm not interested in your view. We'll do what we have to do to protect our town from the likes of you and your fellow south-siders. So pass the message on that none of them are ever welcome over here again.'

'In that case, I'd better leave this here.' Dalton reached into his pocket and Jefferson's belligerent attitude had wound everyone up so much that several people reached for their guns, but when Dalton's hand emerged he was clutching a wad of bills. 'Sheriff Blake gave me a reward for getting Deke.'

'He was an outlaw?'

'Apparently he did some things before he joined up with Paul and Billy. I discussed it with Paul and we agreed that the families of the people he killed should have the money. I took the liberty of keeping some for myself for my troubles and–'

'We have no need for money in Two Forks.'

'I know, but sometimes it can be useful. Whoever wants it is welcome to it.' Dalton held out the wad, but nobody moved towards him. 'If not, I bought tradable goods we could never make or grow ourselves, including medicine, if anyone is interested.'

'We aren't.'

Dalton continued to look along the row of scowling people. He didn't know them well enough to work out which ones were family members of the people Deke had killed. But he was able to identify two of them soon enough. The first was a man who turned on his heel, muttering an oath, then headed back into town. The second man wasn't so reticent and paced up to Dalton.

'Blood money,' he growled then spat on the ground before Dalton's boots. 'Like Jefferson said – I want no part of it.'

With that pronouncement, the northsiders disbanded and headed away, although Jefferson and several others stayed to ensure Dalton left.

As this encounter had gone even worse than he'd feared, Dalton hoped that his first meeting with Loren wouldn't turn out badly, but he needn't have worried.

Loren met him midway between their houses. He reported that he'd seen him riding into the valley and welcomed him back to his house to have a drink and to share news.

For the first time in a while, they sat outside and chatted like the old friends they were. Dalton related the tale of their pursuit of Deke, starting after their argument. Dalton didn't mention Paul's role, but when he came to talking about the reward, Loren's expression became serious.

'And how do you feel about using that money to buy things we don't have here?'

Dalton knew that he wasn't really asking about the reward money, so he considered his answer before replying.

'I don't see nothing wrong about using an unexpected bonus like that reward to buy things that'll make our lives a little easier.' He paused to consider Loren, but couldn't decipher his stern expression. 'But some-times those rewards can't compensate for what we lose by accepting the bonus in the first place.'

Loren continued to look at him and Dalton could tell he was carefully thinking about what he would say.

'I'm glad you think that way,' he said fin-ally. 'That gold nugget would have brought us nothing but disaster, but a reward, ob-tained honestly for a difficult task well done is different.'

'Although the result was as bad as you reckoned it'd be. Nobody wanted their share of the money.'

Loren laughed then leaned forward and winked at Dalton.

'You buy any coffee with that reward money?'

'Sure did.'

'Then I'll bet you a tin against anything you like that you'll get to hand over that money to the northsiders before the week is out.'

'I'll take that bet. Those people were mighty adamant.'

'Jefferson is adamant. I spent a week with them searching for Deke and none of the others are as suspicious of everything we do as he is.'

Cheered by this thought and with their disagreement now smoothed over, Dalton then confided in Loren, telling him the truth about Paul and Billy.

'Durando is a lawless hellhole,' Loren said. 'It's no surprise to me that Sheriff Blake just rounded up the nearest men to a body. Finding anyone who'd know or care about Zachary's murder will be a near impossible task.'

'But a worthwhile one. You don't meet many good men, and Paul is such a man.'

'And Billy is a good lad. He's been making himself as useful as he can with a busted leg and he's determined to repay everyone for their help. Then he wants to settle down here. And it does you credit that you want to help them, but before you do that, I reckon you need to help yourself with one matter.' Loren took a deep breath. 'And that's the one subject I'm surprised you haven't mentioned yet – Eliza.'

Dalton winced. He'd avoided mentioning her, figuring that bad news could wait by which time it might not turn out to be as bad as he'd feared.

'Milo?'

'That one word sums it up.' Loren sighed.

146

'I heard that every day for the first week after you left, he helped her look after Billy, although she, and Billy, didn't need that help. They got mighty friendly. Now he's decided to stay and he's building himself a home.'

Loren pointed down the valley towards a small clearing. Although Dalton had ridden past that clearing, he hadn't seen any sign of a house.

'And he's hoping Eliza will ... will stay with him?'

'I'll put it this way – he doesn't need to find no excuses to visit her no more because she finds plenty of excuses to visit him. So you've got to decide now what you really feel about her.'

'I've been doing plenty of thinking in the last month.' Dalton sighed. 'I already know the answer to that one.'

'Then I just hope it's not too late already.'

Dalton agreed and as he decided he shouldn't waste another moment before acting, he patted his legs and stood.

'Then I'll go. Back in White Falls I bought myself a whole new set of clothes and soap and a present for her. I'll get myself all dandied up and tonight, my friend, I'm going a-courting.'

Loren laughed and slapped him on the back.

'Then I wish you luck, and I expect a full report in the morning.'

As it was, Dalton didn't get the chance to dandy himself up for another hour as half of Loren's prediction came true faster than even he had anticipated.

Dalton returned to his house and waiting for him was the man who had turned on his heel and stormed away earlier when he'd mentioned the reward money. He was standing beside Dalton's horse and eyeing the bulging sacks with interest.

Without undue comment Dalton gave him $100, half the remaining reward money, then asked him if there was anything else he wanted. The man didn't delay in providing a list and in silence he took a sack of corn, a jar of coffee and a saw. He loaded these items onto the back of his horse then turned to lead it away, but he stopped and spoke without looking back at Dalton.

'Deke Grant killed my son James,' he said. 'I'm Sam Taylor.'

Then he left without further comment. The second man, who had even more vehemently rejected Dalton's offer, arrived half an hour later. He also collected his share of the reward money and provided a list of several items he wanted. He did this without any undue comment or sign of approval on his stern face. Neither did he go so far as to share his name, but he provided something that was even more welcome.

'I don't believe in no charity,' he said when he was ready to leave. 'So you make sure you think about what you want to trade for these items. Then let me know.'

'I'd like to do that,' Dalton said. 'But where can I see you? I'm not exactly welcome on the north side of town.'

'Don't worry. I'll see you when I can.' The man favoured him with a wink then left.

Dalton took both encounters as being proof that Loren was right and that Jefferson's attitude about the southsiders wasn't so stridently held amongst the others. So in a happier frame of mind than he'd been in for some time, he put his mind to his most pressing issue – Eliza.

He lit a fire, ferried water from the river, heated it then poured it into a water barrel. Then on the stretch of land before his door he treated himself to a bath. He soaked himself thoroughly removing all trace of trail dust, building up a great lather with the soap. He dosed his hair in a pungent lacquer and after a moment's thought sprinkled a liberal dose on his chest and arms.

Then he dressed himself in his new clothes and pocketed his gift for Eliza – a thin gold chain. He had set his heart on making a gold trinket for her and although he didn't know who had stolen his nugget, he hadn't lost all hope of reclaiming it one day. So he figured that as the fine chain required more skill to make than he'd ever have, it would be a good substitute. And if he ever found his nugget, he could make a trinket and hang it on the chain.

Paul arrived as he was about to set off and after inspecting him and declaring him fit for the task ahead, he suggested he pick a handful of early spring flowers. With Paul's good-natured encouragement ringing in his ears, he set off for Eliza's house.

Halfway down the valley he noticed a fine spiral of smoke rising from her house and as Newell and most of the others were still in the fields, he took that as a sign she was there. Even better, he caught a glimpse of Milo ahead, heading towards the clearing. If Milo noticed him he didn't show it and he disappeared into the trees.

He was intrigued to find out what kind of house Milo was building and so he followed him. The industrial sounds of chopping and sawing started up, letting him locate his quarry. So Dalton took a circuitous route through the trees to come out behind the house. From a small rise he saw that it was almost complete. There would be many rooms inside, all set out around a central room that would look down the valley and, perhaps by accident, away from Dalton's and Loren's house further up the valley.

Despite Milo having had only a month to build it, the house was already larger and finer than Dalton's house. This wasn't a house that one man would build for himself. This was a large family home for a large family.

Dalton was already determined to make the most of tonight's visit with Eliza, but this helped to strengthen his resolve. He slipped away from the house, planning to retrace his steps, but then backed into and almost fell over a mound. He hadn't noticed it when he'd crept closer to the house and he rested a hand on the mound to stop himself falling then stepped back to consider it.

The mound had been handmade, presumably by Milo, and was four feet high and rounded. A tunnel had been bored into the side. Ashes lay within and the fire had burnt the entrance. With there being a hole in the top of the mound, Dalton deduced that Milo had used it to burn something, perhaps at a high temperature.

He fingered the ashes inside, finding that Milo had burnt paper but that there was little that was discernible other than a small oval photograph. Dalton could just make out a woman's face seen in profile and the initials 'CW' scrawled beneath the portrait, but when he tried to pick it up, it crumbled away. There were other burnt pictures and documents in the mound, but he decided not to waste time pondering on what he'd been burning. Milo's activities were of no interest to him any longer, he decided, and in a few hours neither would they interest Eliza any longer.

He set off down the valley. The spiral of smoke coming from Eliza's house was thicker by the time he arrived in town and the enticing aroma of cooking seeped into his nostrils. He hadn't realized how hungry he was until that moment and his mouth watered. She must be cooking for herself and Newell, and he hoped she'd made enough for another mouth, and that Newell would take a hint and eat his dinner quickly and leave.

He saw her in the window, moving around as if she was still cooking, or perhaps cleaning. Despite the strong reflections on the window, he was sure he saw her flinch. Then she put a hand to her brow and hurried to the door.

'Howdy!' he called as the door swung open and she appeared in the doorway.

She didn't reply immediately, looking at him with an odd quizzical expression and not with the usual smile that she had once always provided him.

'You're all spruced up,' she said, frowning.

He stopped and turned on the spot, showing her his suit.

'Sure am.'

'And you're looking most....' Eliza rocked her head from side to side as she considered him, that smile appearing for the first time.

'Clean?' He paced up to her and to avoid being too forward straight away, thrust the flowers into her hand. Then he slipped inside.

She followed him in and they stood awkwardly looking at each other. She turned away, her cheeks reddening, perhaps in embarrassment, and placed the flowers in a water bowl, then on the table, then in the bowl again. Then she rummaged for something more permanent to put them in, taking more time than she ought to.

Dalton took her flustered state as a good sign and he decided to wait until she'd calmed down before he embarked on his carefully rehearsed speech.

When she'd dealt with the flowers, she returned to the bowl and dried her hands on a cloth, which was lying on the table. Instead of wiping her hands with it, she used the strange method of dabbing her hands on the folded cloth, leaving it lying on the table. This was such an unusual action that Dalton looked at her hands, wondering if she'd hurt herself. When he didn't see anything wrong, he looked at the cloth.

He saw her smooth the cloth before she turned to him and Dalton was sure she had hastily covered something up underneath it, but she recovered her composure quickly and smiled.

'It sure is good to see you,' she said.

Dalton detected warmth in her tone and so he decided this was as good a time as any to make his speech. In truth he'd rather face a man like Deke again than say a few personal and emotional words to her, but he took a deep breath, determined to get this over with quickly.

'I've been mighty distracted ever since we first met, what with one disaster happening then another,' he said, speaking so quickly the words ran into each other. 'But now I reckon all the bad times are behind us and I hope we can make a fresh start, together.'

Eliza gulped. Her mouth dropped open.

'Oh!' she murmured.

Dalton couldn't decide whether her surprise was a good sign or not, or whether she was encouraging or discouraging him to continue. To cover up his confusion he paced around the room and let the pleasant smell of her cooking relax him. He stopped before the fire and considered the bubbling pot.

'Now it sure has been a long time since I tasted your cooking. Newell must be looking forward to this meal.'

'Newell isn't,' she whispered. Her tone was guarded and Dalton caught the implication, but he gritted his teeth to mask his disappointment and turned, just managing to keep his expression pleasant and unconcerned.

'You can't be planning to eat all of this on your own.'

'I'm not.' She turned and headed to the window. She fiddled with the cloth then folded it neatly and placed it back on the table. 'Milo is coming for dinner.'

'Milo is coming,' Dalton repeated, unable to think of anything else to say, 'for dinner.'

'And he'll be here soon. It might be best if you ... I think that...'

'I get the idea. I'll be in the way.'

'It's not like that,' she breathed, registering some emotion, perhaps disappointment, perhaps embarrassment. 'It's just that you've been away and I didn't exactly know whether...'

She looked out the window, but Dalton noticed that her gaze had again taken in the folded cloth. As he considered the set of her back, Dalton couldn't decide whether she was looking out the window to avoid looking at him, or to avoid looking at the cloth.

Although she hadn't said the words, she was clearly telling him that as he'd taken so long to make his feelings known, she'd turned to another man. And he took her embarrassment as a further sign that she'd never have considered Milo if he had told her about his feelings earlier.

There were many things he wanted to say to her: things he'd rehearsed on the way back to Two Forks; things he'd thought about while getting ready to come here, and he knew there would be things he would wish he'd said later. Worse, when he thought through what he'd said so far he realized he hadn't actually said anything that would encourage her to choose him.

Despite all this, right now he was tongue-tied and so he fixed his gaze on the cloth, as if it held the answer to his problems. He joined her by the window and they both looked outside, neither person speaking until Dalton flinched then looked down at the cloth as if he'd seen it for the first time.

Then he moved his hand towards it slowly. She didn't react at first, but when his hand touched it, she lunged for it.

Dalton also lunged and, for a moment that might have been comic in other circumstances, they tugged on the cloth. Neither of them was able to drag it closer. Then the cloth slowly unwrapped to reveal the object within that Eliza hadn't wanted him to see before that object fell to the floor, landing with a tinkling clatter.

Eliza uttered a moan of disappointment and dropped to her knees to gather it up. But she was too late. Dalton had seen the flash of gold as the cloth had unravelled. He'd seen the gold pendant lying on the floor and he'd seen her joy as she confirmed it was undamaged.

Worst of all, he knew how she'd come to own it.

Milo Milton had used Loren's idea to make the pendant in a kiln behind his house. But that wasn't as important a concern as the simple fact that there was only one way Milo could have got his hands on that much gold.

Milo had stolen his gold nugget.

CHAPTER 9

'Milo Milton gave you that,' Dalton said, pointing at the gold pendant, now safely folded in the cloth. He just managed to keep his voice calm and free from accusation.

'He did,' Eliza said. 'And I like it very much.'

'But that was my idea,' Dalton muttered, waving his arms in exasperation and biting back the comments he wanted to make. 'I asked you if you'd like something like that before I left.'

'I didn't take you seriously. I mean, how would you ever get your hands on gold?'

'Not any more I can't,' Dalton murmured.

'What do you mean?'

'Nothing.' He knew he wasn't arguing his case very well, but he was too annoyed to tell Eliza the truth right now. 'I guess I didn't think Milo was the kind of man who could get his hands on gold either.'

'He said he had some small gold objects. He built a mould and a kiln at the back of his house.'

'How inventive.'

'I thought so, and I wasn't impressed just because it's gold, but because he was the one who took the time to make something for me.'

Her accusation sapped him of any desire to continue with this argument. She wasn't the person he was annoyed with. He briefly weighed up the possible effect of telling her how Milo had acquired the gold, but this visit had already gone so badly, he doubted it would help.

He bade her goodbye and left, not meeting her eye again, then walked purposefully towards Milo's new house. Every step closer to the house firmed his commitment to the fact that even if he'd been unable to confide in Eliza, he sure wouldn't waste a moment in telling Milo exactly what he thought of him.

He found Milo collecting spring flowers from around his house and Dalton couldn't help but notice he'd already gathered a bigger and more colourful bunch than his own had been. Milo studiously avoided noticing him until he had an overflowing handful then favoured him with a bored glance and a quizzical raised eyebrow.

Dalton unbuttoned then slapped his jacket on the ground at his feet.

'Step over my jacket,' he said, backing away a pace.

Milo glanced at the jacket. 'Why would I want to do that?'

'To get this started. Step over it.'

'I will do no such thing.' Milo grinned as he moved to walk by Dalton, some ten yards to his side. 'I have an intriguing dinner engagement with a very beguiling woman.'

'I know that and one way or another you will step over my jacket before you try to go for that meal.'

Milo stopped, looked ahead for a few seconds then paced round to stand on the other side of the jacket to Dalton.

'And what happens then?'

'And then we'll find out whether you'll have enough teeth left to eat that meal.'

Milo nodded slowly, then with an unconcerned expression on his face he placed the flowers on the ground and arranged them into a pile with far too much care. Then he took a long and slow pace over the jacket.

'There,' he said, spreading his hands and favouring Dalton with a wide grin. 'I've stepped over your new jacket and I've still got all my teeth.'

Dalton considered Milo's gleaming teeth

161

then bunched a fist and advanced on him with determination to obliterate that grin boiling in his blood. Milo stood his ground, but he didn't raise his fists and merely looked at the advancing Dalton without concern in his eyes.

If anything this just served to annoy Dalton even more and he paced up to him to stand toe to toe. He expected Milo to have a retaliatory plan in mind and that he'd find out what that plan was soon enough. But Milo merely met his gaze and so Dalton decided to get to it straight away and find out what he was up against. He hurled back his fist then drove it into Milo's mouth sending him tumbling to the ground.

Milo lay on his back, fingering his bloodied and split lip, then slowly got to his feet and stood with his body hunched forwards and his arms dangling. Dalton delivered a swinging uppercut to Milo's jaw that stood him straight and a round-armed blow to his ear that sent him reeling sideways.

This time Milo stuck out a leg and avoided falling over. So Dalton paced round to stand before him and thumped him in the stomach, making him bleat with pain and stagger around on the spot until he kicked him in the rump and sent him tumbling to his knees.

Milo knelt doubled over clutching his belly then slowly toppled over to lie on his side. Dalton stood over him, feeling curiously unsatisfied. He felt justified in his actions after Milo had stolen from him, but he hadn't expected him not to defend himself.

'Get up and fight!' Dalton demanded.

Milo just lay on the ground, groaning, until Dalton again demanded that he move. Milo looked up then darted his gaze over Dalton's shoulder. This made Dalton glance back and he saw Loren and Paul hurrying into the clearing.

'Leave him!' Loren and Paul shouted together.

'Can't do that,' Dalton said, although in deference to his friends' request he did take a step backwards from Milo.

Loren looked Dalton up and down, no doubt taking in his new clothes, then at the dishevelled and battered Milo lying on the ground.

'I don't need to hear an explanation of why you're doing this,' he said, 'but whatever the reason, beating Milo ain't the answer.'

'And I reckon it is,' Dalton said. 'He made a gold pendant for Eliza.'

Dalton looked at Loren until with a steady

nod Loren acknowledged the full implications of this statement. Then he turned back to Milo.

'So now that we both know what you've done, get up so I can hit you again.'

'I'm not fighting you,' Milo murmured, his words hard to decipher through his rapidly swelling lips.

'Then don't defend yourself, but I'm sure beating you until you give me back what you stole.'

Only when Dalton uttered his last word did Milo react, flinching badly and gulping. Slowly he pushed himself up so that he was kneeling then looked up at him rubbing his ribs and wincing.

'I don't know what you mean.' Milo staggered to his feet and teetered a stumbled pace towards Dalton. 'I haven't stolen Eliza. Well, at least not yet. Maybe after we've had our dinner I might steal her – not that she was yours to steal anyhow.'

'She was,' Dalton roared as with renewed anger surging through his veins he advanced on Milo.

Despite Milo's refusal to defend himself, he slammed both his fists together and swung them like an axe into Milo's cheek, sending him rolling to the ground. Then he loomed over him, waiting for him to get up so that he could hit him again.

'Dalton!' Paul shouted, advancing on him from behind. Firm arms wrapped themselves around his waist and moved to drag him away. 'That's enough. You've got to let Milo go for that meal.'

'I can't,' Dalton murmured, but already he could feel the fight going out of him. He had come here to work off his anger, but with Milo not retaliating, he found he wasn't up to confronting Paul too.

While he let Paul pull him away from Milo, Loren cocked a thumb in the direction of Two Forks, signifying to Milo that he should go. Milo took an inordinate amount of time to get to his feet then collected his hat and gathered up his bunch of flowers. He slowly straightened, wincing as he flexed his back.

'You sure hurt me plenty with those fists of yours,' he said.

'You deserved it, and remember this: I can beat you again any time I choose.'

'I'm sure you can.' Milo rolled his shoulders then winced again and fingered his jaw, then his split lips. 'Just as I can beat you any time I choose.'

Dalton considered the bruises already

165

emerging on Milo's face and snorted.

'One look at your face will convince any-one that's another lie.'

'There are more ways to win a fight than by inflicting bruises.' Milo stood tall. 'But I don't mind receiving a few from you. Eliza is a mighty fine healer and I reckon she'll enjoy rubbing ointment into my wounds.'

Dalton considered Milo's lopsided grin and in a stunned moment realized the truth. Milo had deliberately lost the fight to get himself hurt. Already he could imagine how Eliza would react to the story of how he'd beaten him.

'Why you–' Dalton said, advancing on Milo, but this time Loren grabbed his shoulders and dragged him back. Dalton struggled but found that Loren had a firm grip of him. 'That man is not going to see Eliza and tell her even more lies.'

'He is,' Loren said, 'and you and I need to talk. When you've calmed down, you can decide what you're going to do about him.'

Dalton knew that Loren was talking sense, but he still struggled while Milo took his time in leaving. So Loren asked Paul to escort Milo out of the clearing and make sure he didn't come back.

Only when the two men had left the

clearing did Dalton relax then bid Loren to release him. He turned to face him and spread his hands.

'Loren, you know I have to stop him seeing Eliza. But I'm still mighty angry about this. Will you come with me and make sure I do this right?'

'Do what right? He's entitled to fight for her in any way he chooses. Letting you beat him to a pulp was an odd way of doing it, but I'm kind of impressed by his commitment.'

'I don't mean that. I mean the gold. Someone stole my gold nugget and as it wasn't Deke, it was someone from Two Forks. And now Eliza has a gold pendant that he made for her.'

'How did he say he got the gold?'

Dalton rubbed his jaw and delivered a rueful sigh.

'I didn't exactly give him a chance to answer that, but Eliza said he made it from some other gold he happened to have.'

Loren winced. 'And did it occur to you that he might have done just that?'

'Nope.'

Loren shook his head as he placed a hand on Dalton's shoulder.

'This is just the kind of problem I tried to

warn you about. Before you found the gold, you were contented. Now, it's caused you so many problems you've probably lost Eliza.'

'It's only a problem because Milo stole it.' Dalton slammed his hands on hips. 'And that varmint ain't getting away with it. When Eliza finds out–'

'Be quiet!' Loren roared, his voice echoing in the clearing. His sudden anger quietened Dalton before he continued in a softer voice. 'Milo didn't steal your precious nugget.'

'How can you know that for sure?'

'I can,' Loren said, not meeting Dalton's eye, 'because I was the one who took it.'

CHAPTER 10

'You stole my gold!' Dalton said, aghast.

'Not stole,' Loren said. 'I took your gold while you were down in Two Forks to work out how I could make it into a ring, but then I kept it to–'

'Stole or took or kept, I still got to ask why?'

'I think you know the answer to that. Like I told you – gold does something bad to a man's soul and no good could come out of you having found it.'

Dalton was speechless for several seconds before he could blurt out a response.

'You're right. It made my friend take something that wasn't his.'

Loren sighed. 'I was only giving you some time to think things through.'

'Some time! You let me go all the way down to White Falls on the assumption that Deke Grant took the nugget.'

'That worked out fine in the end.'

'Do not insult me by telling me you did it for my own good.'

Loren ventured a smile. 'Then I won't. I'm sorry. I shouldn't have done it and you can have it back any time you want, but I'd just hoped you'd find you didn't want it.'

'That was my decision to make, but you didn't understand me. I didn't want it for any other reason than to make something nice to give to Eliza, and now you've made sure I've lost her.'

Loren didn't look him in the eye. Perhaps he was offended that Dalton was accusing him of doing something that wasn't completely his fault, but right now, Dalton was too annoyed to care what his feelings were.

'Like I told you,' Loren said, his voice sad. 'When you want it back just come and see me.'

Loren turned and headed out of the clearing. Dalton watched him leave and he couldn't help but think he wouldn't see him again.

The following days passed slowly. Paul was initially irritated that Dalton hadn't told him about the missing nugget, although the more pressing need to clear his name drove that irritation from his mind.

If Dalton had followed Loren back to his house to reclaim his nugget on the night of their argument, things could have quickly got back to normal. As it was, he hadn't done that and so each passing day made it harder for him to go and see him. He put his faith in the hope that they would meet accidentally and then find a way to smooth over their disagreement. But with Loren going off on a hunting trip, they didn't get that chance.

Dalton stopped making his daily visits to Two Forks and so he didn't see Eliza or Milo. Neither did he see Jefferson Parker, although he did meet other northsiders who came to his house to trade. Each person didn't stay for longer than was necessary to complete their business and neither did they dally to chat, but they were cordial.

Dalton would have welcomed the same level of cordiality from the southsiders. Eliza viewed Dalton's beating of Milo as badly as Dalton had feared. Not that she told him this. She was so annoyed that Newell came to see him and reported on his sister's behalf that she didn't want to see him again.

Dalton couldn't think of any reason why she should take a different view and he accepted her decision with as much good grace as possible.

Billy also moved out of Eliza and Newell's

171

house and joined Paul in staying with him. He told him more details of what had happened between Eliza and Milo in the month while he'd been away and in the days after his disastrous homecoming. None of those details cheered Dalton into thinking he'd ever get close to her again.

In compensation, Paul and Billy proved to be pleasant company. Both men were easygoing and they settled into a comfortable living arrangement. Further down the valley, Milo continued to build his house. When the wind was in the wrong direction, his industrious sounds were audible from Dalton's house and provided a consistent reminder of his troubles. But soon the need to move on to Durando started to dominate his thoughts. Billy wasn't up to completing the journey and although Dalton had hoped Loren would join them, he had to admit that was now unlikely.

Spring was warming the air on the day when Dalton and Paul prepared to set off on the journey, but while Dalton was giving Billy his last instructions for looking after his property, Newell arrived.

'I've got news,' he said then pointed down the valley. 'Loren is back and he wants you to hear what he has to say. He thought it best if Billy and Paul were there to hear it too.'

Dalton had hoped for something like this to happen, but now that it had, it didn't cheer him. He sighed.

'Seems as if things are still so bad between us, he needs you to act as an intermediary.'

Newell offered a brief smile. 'I'm glad to if it gets you two talking again.'

Dalton acknowledged the sense of this with a rueful nod and along with Paul and Billy they headed down into the valley. Billy always used any opportunity to walk and so they set off on foot. He was able to walk at a reasonable pace, but even so Newell walked even slower and, guessing that he wanted to talk to him alone, Dalton slowed to join him.

They had passed Milo's house when Newell spoke up.

'Eliza gets married at the end of the month,' he said.

Ahead, Paul glanced back, having clearly heard this comment, then encouraged Billy to speed his walking.

'Don't suppose I'm surprised,' Dalton said. 'Obliged that you told me.'

'I didn't tell you for your own good, but as a warning. I'd expected that when Eliza wed it'd be to you and that was fine with me. But

173

recently I've lost faith in you being the right man for her. Now I don't want you doing … doing anything untoward.'

'Like beating on Milo again?'

'Like that.'

'But he's not the right man for her. There's just something plain wrong about him.'

'If you're right, then Eliza is making a mistake, but it's hers to make and I won't have you ruining her life, and ours.'

'Ours?'

'I went to see Jefferson Parker yesterday. He has the right to marry people and I wanted everything to be done properly for my sister. Things have worked out as I expected they would. A month apart without trouble has mellowed him. We spoke civilly and if this wedding goes off fine, it'll be another step towards reconciling the town. I don't want you causing trouble and jeopardizing that.'

'Like we once said to each other – we both have to do what we think is right.' With that statement, Dalton paced on ahead to join Paul and Billy.

They spoke no more about the matter as they headed down to Eliza's house. In truth, Dalton had no idea what the right thing to do was. But he did know that he'd ensure he got back from Durando before the wedding then find a reason to confront Milo again and this time somehow prove he wasn't right for Eliza.

When they reached the house, Billy sat on the bench beside the door to rest his leg. Newell went in to fetch Loren and he emerged with both Eliza and Milo. They'd linked arms. Dalton hadn't spoken to Eliza since the fight, but he decided this wasn't the time to do anything other than to be civil.

Milo considered him while sporting his usual smile that Dalton chose to see as a self-satisfied smirk and he hugged Eliza with a tighter hold than was necessary. Dalton didn't meet his gaze and instead looked at Loren, hoping that what he had to say would help to heal the rift between them.

Loren paced back and forth several times, not looking at Dalton and coming to a halt with him facing Paul and Billy.

'I thought it best that Dalton should know that two days ago I met Sheriff Rory Blake up in the hills.' Despite addressing Dalton, Loren kept his gaze on Paul and Billy.

Dalton flinched and this caught Newell's and Eliza's attention, only everyone's positions stopping them from noticing that Billy paled and that Paul reached out to place a hand on his shoulder. Dalton was unsure why Loren had volunteered this information in such a public way, but he hoped it was to give everyone sufficient time to consider what they did next.

'Was he heading this way?' Dalton asked.

'He was going to Durando,' Loren said, still not looking at him, 'but I talked with him and he's planning to come here afterwards.'

As Dalton considered this information, Eliza spoke up.

'Why did you need us to hear this?'

'Good question,' Milo grumbled before Loren could answer. 'Except I haven't got the time to waste to hear it.'

He turned on his heel and left, pacing into the house quickly. Eliza shot Dalton an accusatory glance, suggesting she thought he'd left to avoid being in Dalton's company.

'Because we rarely get newcomers,' Loren said, 'and I thought you should know the sheriff might come, and because he might want to question Dalton some more. Same might go for Paul and Billy.'

Newell and Eliza accepted this information without further comment and with nobody saying anything more, Loren bade his goodbyes and headed off. Dalton considered hurrying on to ask him for more details, but settled for being pleased that they had spoken civilly and for hoping that would break the ice for their next meeting. Billy chose to remain sitting a while longer to rest his leg, and perhaps give himself time to think, so he walked back with Paul. Not surprisingly neither man was talkative. Eventually Paul broke the silence.

'You reckon we should still go to Durando?' he asked.

'I reckon your best chance is to act on your own terms. Waiting here for Sheriff Blake to find you won't help to prove your innocence.'

'It's a long journey there and back. We might miss that wedding.'

Dalton snorted. 'If there is one.'

Paul laughed. 'I'd gathered you'd do something to stop Milo marrying her. If there's anything I can do to help before we leave, just ask.'

Dalton stopped and considered Paul.

'Actually, there is. You were so busy being shocked and feeling guilty at the mention of Rory Blake's name that you missed something important, something that everyone else missed.' Dalton raised his eyebrows.

'Milo Milton was even more shocked than you were.'

'Was he?' Paul murmured. 'I didn't see that.'

'I can't work out whether Loren ensured we were all standing in the right positions so that I'd see that when nobody else did, but either way I was looking at Milo. He flinched away from Eliza, kneaded his brow, then stopped himself stumbling by putting a hand on the wall. Then he made his excuses and slipped away. For a man who always acts so calmly, that wasn't like him.'

Paul looked back down the valley towards Two Forks.

'What can he be so worried about?'

'I don't know, but I'm hoping it's because he's got a guilty conscience.' Dalton pointed to Milo's house. 'And I reckon we should find out why.'

Five minutes later they stood outside Milo's house and Dalton had prised open the shutters to the largest window.

'You sure we should do this now?' Paul asked.

'Milo is with Eliza,' Dalton said. 'He won't be back for hours.'

Paul nodded and so together they slipped in through the window.

'So what are we looking for?'

'Something, anything, everything.' Dalton looked around. 'But I know one thing for sure – something in here's got to prove Milo is up to no good.'

Paul nodded and so they set about their searching the house. The sun was at its highest by the time Dalton admitted defeat.

They had been as thorough as they could be while keeping everything they touched in an undisturbed state, but there hadn't been much to search through and none of it had been incriminating. They had just found clothes and a few other belongings.

'Well,' Paul said as they slipped out the window, 'if he is up to no good, we'll have to find another way to prove it.'

'Now that's the kind of thinking I like.'

Cheered by Paul's enthusiasm after their failure, Dalton stepped back from the house and looked it over one last time. His gaze passed over the house, the corral at the side, and ended at the wagon. Two months ago an argument over this wagon had helped to start off a disastrous series of events and with a last hope tapping at his mind, Dalton headed to the wagon.

A rough blanket lay on the back and when Dalton threw the blanket back, he revealed a bag. Paul smiled and jumped onto the wagon ahead of Dalton and opened the bag, but it was empty. He tipped it upside-down and shook it but still nothing emerged, and so the two men sat on the back of the wagon with their feet dangling, contemplating their failure.

'We ought to go soon before he comes back,' Paul said, still peering into the bag in the forlorn hope that it'd contain something they could use against him.

'We won't,' Dalton said, eyeing the bag with more interest than Paul was.

'We can't confront him when we don't have anything on him.'

'But we have, and this bag proves what he did.'

'There's nothing in it.'

'There isn't.' Dalton took the bag and turned it round so that Paul could see the monogrammed initials on the front. 'But what's on the outside is sure interesting.'

'ZJ,' Paul said, reading the inscription, 'but who is...?'

Paul's eyes opened wide as the only possible answer as to who owned this unusual set of initials dawned on him.

'Doctor Zachary Jones,' Dalton said. 'The man you were supposed to have killed.'

'That could just be a huge coincidence.'

Dalton detected from Paul's encouraging tone that he wanted to believe and wanted Dalton to convince him.

'Then think about this – Zachary Jones was a doctor and when Milo Milton arrived he saved Billy's leg using a technique he'd learnt from a friend from Durando.'

Paul winced. 'I got bad news then. Zachary Jones wasn't a doctor as such. He pulled teeth.'

'Then perhaps that piece of the puzzle is wrong but I reckon Milo killed Zachary for the gold he had.' Dalton shrugged. 'Perhaps for making gold teeth, or perhaps from a locket that once contained this picture I found.'

'That is just a theory and not fact.'

'True, but Milo got agitated at the mention of Rory Blake's name and at the very least, we've got a starting point to take Milo on now and a starting point to prove your innocence.'

Paul considered for a few moments then gave a slow nod.

Their attack was precise and effective.

It came two hours after sundown when Milo was returning to his house. He was whistling a merry tune under his breath when in the poor light Paul stepped out from the bushes in front of him. This made Milo flinch and stop below an oak. Paul called out to Milo in a pleasant tone, confirming he had nothing to worry about, but when Milo took another pace forward, Dalton dropped out of the tree. He caught Milo around the shoulders, bundling him to the ground. Paul stepped forward and helped him pin Milo down.

They frisked him, confirming he was unarmed, then gagged him, threw a blanket over his head, and trussed him up. Then they dragged him back to his house and threw him into the back of his wagon. Ten minutes later they were heading away from Two Forks at a fair pace.

Only when they were five miles out of town and there was no chance that anyone could hear Milo's shouts for help, if they came, did they stop and remove the gag from Milo's mouth. In the darkness Dalton could see only Milo's outline and he couldn't make out his expression, but from his bright eyes he didn't judge him to be panicking.

'I should have realized,' Milo said, 'that you'd do something like this. Some people just can't accept they've been beaten by the better man.'

'You're wrong on both counts, Milo Milton, if that is your name.'

This was a guess, but it did cause Milo to narrow his eyes.

'What you getting at?'

Dalton collected the bag from the back of the wagon then slapped it into Milo's chest.

'I mean Sheriff Rory Blake was looking for Deke Grant because he reckoned he killed Zachary Jones, but I reckon he got the wrong man.'

Milo glanced at the bag then shrugged away from it and when he spoke his confident words didn't correspond with his nervous tone.

'And all you have on me is a bag with some initials on it that just happen to be the same as a dead man's.'

Dalton hadn't drawn Milo's attention to the initials and so he judged Milo's comment as another sign of his guilt.

'I have plenty more evidence and you know what it is.' In truth he didn't have much more than this bag, a hunch, and a grudge, but he fixed him with his gaze and he was pleased that Milo looked away.

'You're making the worst mistake of your life, Dalton,' Milo said finally. 'And it'll be your last.'

Dalton ignored him and signified to Paul that he should gag him. Then they climbed into the front of the wagon and without further comment headed up into hills, gaining as much distance from Two Forks as they could on the first night of their journey.

The next morning Milo was composed and again protested his innocence. Dalton didn't believe him, although he did encourage him to talk, hoping he might inadvertently reveal something incriminating. He didn't but whenever they stopped for a break, he removed his gag and chatted with him. But each time Milo only repeated his statement that they'd regret what they were doing.

Dalton wasn't concerned. He had seen how nervous Milo had been when he'd first heard Sheriff Blake was nearby and he judged his confidence to be an act. So he responded with the same level of calmness as Milo always showed, then replaced his gag.

With their prisoner trussed up on the back of the wagon, they set about locating the lawman.

It took them three days to find signs of a recent group of riders heading towards

Durando, which they presumed was Rory and his men. Two days later – and six days out of Durando – they caught their first sight of him. He was riding with three men, presumably deputies.

As they'd agreed earlier, they took the wagon and their prisoner into the trees. Then Dalton approached Rory on his own. He was four-hundred yards away when Rory saw him and he stopped on the trail then bade him approach with a friendly bellow of encouragement.

'Dalton,' he shouted when Dalton was closer. 'I do declare. I'd planned to see you later, but you found me first. What do you want?'

Rory's cheerful demeanour pleased Dalton, proving to him that they were right to come to him first in an open manner.

'It's a long story,' Dalton said, stopping ten yards back from the lawmen, 'but it's a true one. It concerns the man who killed Zachary Jones.'

Rory smiled, looking round at his men and encouraging them to share his good humour.

'I thought that five-hundred dollar reward would intrigue you. What you found?'

'I don't want a reward this time and I reckon you won't want to give me one anyhow.' Dalton lowered his voice, giving it a serious tone. 'I lied to you when I last saw you. Deke Grant didn't ride into Two Forks alone. Paul Stark and Billy Boyd were with him.'

Rory accepted this information with barely a flicker in his smile.

'And the reason for the lie?'

'Paul and Billy are innocent.'

Rory leaned forward, his jaw firming as his expression became more serious.

'That is only your opinion and you are in deep trouble.' Rory rested his hand on his gunbelt. 'Now tell me where they are or you'll get a reward you'll find a lot less enjoyable than five-hundred dollars.'

'I intend to, but I need to know you'll deal with them fairly and for that matter that you'll also deal with the man who really killed Zachary Jones fairly, because I have him.'

Dalton's final comment made Rory flinch back in his saddle in surprise.

'You are a surprisingly resourceful man.' He gestured down the trail. 'Lead me to them and I'll deal with them all accordingly.'

Dalton couldn't decide whether this meeting had gone well or badly, but having stated his case he saw no reason why he could now not complete on the decision Paul and he had agreed upon before they'd kidnapped Milo.

He leaned back and gestured. Presently Paul drove the wagon out of the trees. Rory narrowed his eyes to confirm the identity of the approaching man then glanced around at his deputies and gave a small gesture. Dalton judged that his silent order was telling them to be on their guard for trouble.

'Paul will give you no problems,' Dalton said. 'He's not the man you reckon he is. If you trust me, you should accept him. The same can't be said for our prisoner.'

Rory said nothing in reply as he watched Paul pull up the wagon at Dalton's side. Paul kept his hands held high as he stood and climbed into the back of the wagon then dragged Milo to a sitting position. Milo looked at Rory without concern in his eyes and when Paul whipped off his gag, Milo was grinning.

'That's your suspect, is it?' Rory said then snorted in disbelief.

'Yeah,' Dalton said. 'This is Milo Milton and he killed Zachary Jones.'

Rory considered this information then looked around at his men and nodded. A moment before his deputies reacted, Dalton noticed Milo's grin widen, his demeanour showing a level of unconcern that was beyond arrogance.

Then as one of Rory's deputies drew their guns. One deputy moved his horse in and scooped Dalton's gun away then slammed the barrel of his gun against Dalton's neck. Paul started to shout something, his hand twitching towards his holster, but his hand didn't reach his gun as the clearing echoed to the sound of gunfire, drowning out his words. Dalton could only watch in horror as repeated gunfire slammed into Paul's chest, his friend dancing a deathly dance before he crashed from the back of the wagon to land on his back.

The deputies took no chances and slammed round after round into his body.

'You'll get the same,' Rory said when they finally relented, 'if you try anything.'

Dalton stared in shocked horror at his friend's dead body.

'Paul did nothing,' he murmured aghast, 'and yet you killed him.'

'Paul shot up my guards when he escaped and I sure as hell wasn't giving him a chance to do that again. You though get one chance to explain your actions.'

'What actions?'

Rory drew his horse closer to Dalton and considered him.

'I checked out your story. You were seen talking with Paul in the saloon. The next day he was seen following you out of town. I sent some deputies after him. They found him, but they ended up dead. You'd better hope you can convince me you had nothing to do with that.'

'The only thing you should be worrying about is Zachary Jones's murder.'

'You don't tell me what to do,' Rory said, pointing an accusing finger at him. Then he gestured to one of his deputies. 'Untie Milo.'

'If you're keeping me prisoner,' Dalton said, 'you have to keep him prisoner too. Check the bag he had on him with Zachary's initials on it.'

'What bag?' Milo said when the deputy had slit through his bonds. He rubbed his wrists then stretched.

'The bag that...' Dalton winced. It had been on the back of the wagon, but while he had left him and Paul to approach the sheriff, Milo would have had the time to throw it over the side.

Dalton looked at Rory then Milo in turn, wondering whether it was worth searching for it, but he noted the smiles they directed to each other, the relaxed nature of their tones when they'd spoken. The worrying truth dawned on him.

'You two know each other,' he murmured.

'Yup,' Rory said. 'Milo was the last person to see Zachary Jones alive. It was his testimony that helped me track down Deke and his gang of varmints.'

'Sure was,' Milo said, jumping down from the wagon. 'I did try to tell you that kidnapping me was a big mistake, Dalton.'

'Don't trust this man,' Dalton said, but aside from the deputy who ordered him to get down from his horse, nobody was paying him any attention. As the deputy directed him to take Milo's place in the wagon, Milo turned to Rory.

'And now,' he said, 'we need to hurry back to Two Forks. The last of Deke's gang Billy Boyd is still there. And I don't want to be late for my wedding.'

CHAPTER 11

'Do not trust Milo Milton,' Dalton said.

Rory looked up from his sullen consideration of the campfire and snorted.

'Be quiet,' he said.

They'd been travelling back towards Two Forks for five days and until now Dalton hadn't had a chance to talk privately with Rory about Milo. But with Milo having gone off into the bushes after their evening meal, Dalton reckoned this might be the last chance he'd get to present his case.

'Milo is a compulsive liar. He's been in Two Forks for a month yet never mentioned he'd seen Deke and the others.'

'He didn't see them. He just saw Zachary. I worked out it was Deke who killed him.'

'What about Paul and Billy?'

'They were with him so I rounded 'em up.'

'From what I heard they were unconscious when the doctor died and without other evidence isn't it just as likely that Milo killed him then lied to cover up what he did?'

'Milo is a decent man. The others aren't.'

'Milo is a natural liar. Everything he says is riddled with falsehoods and one of those lies is sure to unravel if you question him thoroughly.'

Rory pointed a firm finger at him. 'That is enough. Be quiet.'

'I won't when a guilty man is free and you shot up my friend.'

'I shot an escaped prisoner who twice shot up my deputies.'

Dalton lowered his head while he considered what kind of approach might work with Rory. Loren had been right. In a hellhole like Durando, even the law didn't worry too much about the truth when they found a dead body. They just rounded up the live bodies who were nearest to the corpse.

'Then if you won't tell me anything, I'll surmise on my own. I reckon in a town like Durando, the man who killed and robbed Zachary stole gold...' Dalton saw movement and glanced to the side to see that Milo was returning to the camp-fire. He spoke quickly. 'If I knew whether anything of Zachary's had been stolen, I could tell you whether I'd seen it around.'

Rory shrugged. 'I'll discuss that with Billy when I've arrested him.'

Milo was now close enough to hear them talk and he stopped to consider both men.

'Then at least,' Dalton said, 'let me speak to Billy first and make him give himself up. I sure don't want you shooting him up too.'

Rory glared at him but he provided a short nod before turning his back on him. Milo wandered closer to Dalton and smiled.

'Interesting comments you were making there, Dalton,' he said. 'But I reckon if Billy still has the gold he stole off Zachary, he'd be intelligent enough to dispose of it.'

'Or melt it down?'

Milo laughed. 'Perhaps Billy would think of doing that. It'd be sure to destroy the evidence and make it impossible to prove what he really did.'

Despite Milo's gloating, Dalton smiled. Until now there had been a small element of doubt in his mind as to whether he'd let his dislike of Milo cloud his judgement, but this was as good an admission of guilt as he reckoned he'd ever get. It wouldn't help to prove that guilt, but it did at least make his own actions sure.

Dalton returned Milo's smile.

'Difficult,' he said, 'but not impossible.'

It was late in the day when Rory's group

193

arrived in Two Forks. For the last two days Dalton hadn't spoken again with either Milo or Rory, but he didn't need to. His only concerns now were ensuring that Billy didn't suffer the same fate as Paul had and choosing the right moment to take on Milo.

They headed down into the valley, coming out by the river close to the north side of the town. As Dalton expected, their arrival quickly gathered the townsfolk's attention. Sitting on the back of the wagon, Dalton avoided meeting anyone's eye, but he heard everyone's aggrieved comments upon seeing him being taken into town in bonds.

Rory headed around the outskirts of town and as he led his men through the river, they gathered a trailing gaggle of townsfolk, who were all eager to see what happened next. Not surprisingly, the combination of their arrival and the commotion raised by the northsiders wading through the river encouraged the southsiders to leave the fields and head for their homes.

Dalton rolled up from his sitting position to kneel and darted his gaze amongst them, looking for Billy. His first potential sighting was of a distant form breaking away from the main group and hurrying into Eliza's house. From the person's hobbling gait,

Dalton deduced he had to be Billy. Milo murmured a confirmation of his identity to Rory and so Rory shouted out orders for them to speed into town.

Rory hurried his horse on and burst though the milling southsiders then carried on to the house. The other deputies and Milo hurried after him. Dalton couldn't help but notice that several people, including Newell, pointed him out then stared at him with their mouths open in shock, but he avoided meeting their eyes. Instead, he watched Rory draw his horse to a halt around twenty yards away from the house then parade around, presumably checking that the window and door were the only exits.

'You've got one chance to live, Billy,' he shouted. 'Come out now, or die where you stand!'

The house remained silent as Rory waited for the wagon and his deputies to catch up with him. The men dismounted and lined up before the house. Despite their previous agreement, Rory didn't look at Dalton, and so Dalton took it upon himself to act.

'Billy,' he shouted, kneeling on the back of the wagon. 'Like Rory said, come out. I can't promise you you'll get much in the way of justice. But Paul is dead and you will be too if you don't give yourself up.'

Dalton had said his piece and tied up as he was, he could do nothing more than hope Billy would be sensible. He was relieved when Rory nodded to him, but he'd seen how quickly this trigger-happy lawman reacted and he didn't hold out much hope for Billy's chances if he didn't take his advice. To his great relief the door swung open a few inches.

'Paul's dead?' Billy shouted from inside.

'Shot to hell,' Rory said, 'just like you will be unless you come out with those hands reaching for the sky.'

'But he did nothing wrong, like me.'

Rory didn't reply and merely glanced at his deputies, clearly directing them to storm the house when he gave the order.

'Billy,' Dalton shouted. 'You have to come out now. You'll have to fight to prove your innocence, but that's a better chance than you'll get if you stay in there.'

The townsfolk were now closing on them and Dalton reckoned Rory would react within seconds. But to his relief Billy hobbled out, his eyes downcast and his hands thrust high. He looked up to glance around at the arc of guns directed at him, but did nothing but hold his chin high.

Maybe it was the presence of the numerous witnesses or maybe Dalton had misjudged Rory but whatever the reason was, Rory provided a calm gesture to a deputy. This man hurried in and grabbed Billy then frisked him and dragged him towards the wagon. In short order he trussed him up and placed him down to sit beside Dalton, who provided him with an encouraging smile that Billy didn't return.

By the time the deputy had jumped down from the wagon, the townsfolk were congregating around the wagon. Rory identified himself, but while he was stating his reasons for arresting Billy, the encounter Dalton had dreaded happened. Eliza shouted out with relief and hurried towards Milo. He jumped down from his horse and stood with his arms outstretched then gathered her up and swung her round. They embraced, Dalton noting that Milo moved her into a position where he could see them hug each other.

'I've been so worried,' she said, hugging him again. Then she disentangled herself and looked at Billy. 'But why has he arrested Billy?'

'He's suspected of murdering Doctor Zachary Jones in Durando,' Milo said.

'He's not suspected, he did it,' Rory said, then pointed at the wagon. 'I've yet to work out how Dalton fits in with that crime, but he's coming with me too.'

'Dalton?' Eliza murmured, as if she hadn't even realized he was on the wagon.

'I'm sure,' Newell said, joining her, 'Dalton had nothing to do with any murder there. We can all vouch for the fact he's never even been to Durando.'

Before Rory could provide an answer, Milo obligingly spoke up.

'Dalton lied to the lawman,' he said, 'saying Paul and Billy hadn't been here, although he knew both of them were wanted for Zachary's murder. He never mentioned that to anyone here then kidnapped me and tried to frame me for the murder. Luckily, Rory knew the truth and arrested him.'

Despite the growing damning evidence against him, Dalton reckoned he'd made enough friends here to ensure he could rely on some support. But he was less sure about the views of the northsiders who were hurrying closer.

Rory and his deputies formed a line to watch them approach, turning their backs on Newell. Jefferson Parker was leading the group with such a determined tread to his gait and his usual indignation burning from his glowering expression that Rory grunted orders to his men to prepare for trouble. The deputies spread out, ignoring the seemingly innocuous southsiders who were standing behind them.

Dalton didn't pay much attention to anyone but the advancing Jefferson, not expecting that the ineffectual Newell would do anything. And so it was with some surprise that he saw movement and turned to see Newell advancing on Rory from behind.

In a move that he must have co-ordinated while Dalton wasn't looking, he lunged in and tipped Rory's gun out of its holster and while Rory was swirling round to confront him, three other men took on the other deputies. Two deputies found their guns removed then turned on them. Only one deputy managed to avoid an assault but within seconds three men were on him and bundled him to the ground.

Despite the sudden change of fortunes, Rory dropped to one knee and lunged for his gun, but Newell kicked it away. Another man picked it up and turned it on the lawman.

'You'll regret this,' Rory growled, eyeing the arc of townsfolk around him with concentrated hostility burning from his eyes.

'We won't,' Newell said. 'Two Forks folk look after their own, no matter what they've done wrong.'

Newell looked up at the wagon and fixed Dalton with his surprisingly firm gaze. While Dalton acknowledged the stand he had taken by returning a brief smile, Rory muttered threats but then trailed off when Jefferson and the northsiders speeded in to join them.

'Damn southsiders,' Jefferson spluttered. 'You're taking on lawmen now.'

'We're doing nothing wrong,' Newell said. 'Dalton and Billy may have made mistakes, but we'll be the ones who'll judge them. If we reckon the sheriff has a valid case, he can take them away. Otherwise, they stay here. I believe that to be in all our best interests.'

Newell's request for clemency and commonsense only went to annoy Jefferson more and he swirled round to face his fellow northsiders.

'They're all the same. The sooner the law takes them all away the better. They're not content with just eating our food and encouraging outlaws who shoot up our people. Now they're taking on the law. We're not like these animals. We free the lawmen.'

Jefferson stood to one side and beckoned

for the men who had come with him to advance on the held lawmen and free them. For his part, Newell shook his head sadly then murmured instructions to hold on to them no matter what the northsiders did.

For long moments the two sides of the town faced each other and Dalton reckoned the long-suppressed hostility between the two factions would bubble over into a fight, and perhaps with Sheriff Blake being involved, a bloodbath. But nobody moved towards each other. Jefferson shouted out another demand to take on the southsiders, his face suffused to darkness, but when they moved only one man stepped forward, Sam, the man who had first traded with Dalton.

'I don't reckon the law should take Dalton away,' he said. 'We should decide whether he's done wrong here.'

With sudden hope swelling in his mind, Dalton looked around until he identified the other people with whom he'd traded. Presently another man stepped forward to join him, the second person to come to him for goods.

'Dalton is a decent man,' he said. 'We should hear what he has to say.'

'We do not listen to southsiders!' Jefferson roared.

'Then perhaps we should start.'

This simple comment gathered a murmuring of support causing Jefferson to flail his arms and mutter barely audible oaths. Dalton could see his authority seeping away with every tortured and ignored comment. Dalton couldn't tell if this mutiny was taking place because of good feelings towards him or bad feelings towards Jefferson, but either way he was pleased it was happening.

When several more people stepped forward to surround the lawmen and join the southsiders, Newell raised a hand, calling for calm.

'I suggest,' he said, looking at Rory, 'we hold our town meeting now.'

Rory snorted his opposition to this plan, but as he roved his gaze across the determined townsfolk, his shoulders slumped.

'Then do it, but do it quickly and make the right decision.'

Jefferson continued to shout defiant comments, but with Rory having backed down from escalating the confrontation, nobody listened to him.

'I reckon,' Newell said, 'we'd all like to hear Dalton's story first.'

Everyone's gaze turned on him, but Dalton sought out Milo and nodded towards him.

'The man who killed Zachary Jones stole gold,' he said.

'And where is that gold?' Rory asked, his tone sounding bored.

'I'm looking at it right now.' Dalton gestured with his bound hands towards Eliza. 'It's around Eliza's neck, except Milo melted it down to make that pendant.'

Milo let his mouth fall open, appearing aghast as if he'd never heard this accusation before.

'That's preposterous!' he blustered.

'It isn't.' Dalton raised his voice so everyone heard his next comment, his only valid piece of evidence. 'You melted down a locket that once contained a picture of a woman with the initials CW.'

Milo remained glassy eyed, suggesting to Dalton that he was lost for words, and it was Rory who spoke up next.

'Christine Walker,' he said, intrigue lighting his eyes for the first time as he swung round to face Dalton. 'She was Zachary's dead wife. How do you know about her?'

'Because I saw her burnt photograph in Milo's kiln.' In truth, it'd crumbled to dust when he'd touched it, but Milo didn't know that. He took a deep breath, hoping that Milo would panic now.

For long moments nobody said anything until Milo extracted himself from Eliza's arm and paced round to the wagon to look up at Dalton.

'Then show us this burnt photograph,' he said, meeting his gaze, 'and then we can all see who is lying here.'

CHAPTER 12

'Why are you doing this to him?' Billy asked when the wagon on which they were travelling came to a halt outside Milo's house.

'Because Milo is a liar and an evil man,' Dalton said.

'But he saved my life.'

'He did, but using skills he learnt from the man he killed.'

Billy shook his head in disbelief and turned away, leaving Dalton to slip off the back of the wagon to await the verdict. At Newell's request, Rory had removed his bonds, but he didn't expect his free status to last for long if Rory didn't find the evidence he had promised was in Milo's kiln.

The entire town had traipsed up the valley to see the result of the search. Whatever the rights and wrongs of Rory taking Billy and Dalton back to White Falls, everything rested on what Rory found.

Jefferson Parker stood at the back of the group, glowering at everyone's backs and Dalton guessed that the success of Newell's sudden attempt to exert authority also rested on the outcome of Rory's search. If Dalton turned out to be wrong, Jefferson would perhaps be free to spread his poisonous views and convince the northsiders of the problems that resulted from siding with the southsiders.

Dalton offered Newell an encouraging smile that didn't reflect his feelings then glanced at the confident Milo, who was watching Rory pace towards the kiln with eager anticipation. Dalton crossed his fingers in the hope that amongst the ashes he would find some of Zachary's documents that had not been burnt to ashes. But he had seen them over a week ago and he had to admit he'd put his faith into something that increasingly felt like the wrong way of proving Milo was a liar.

Sure enough, Rory quickly turned away from the kiln and returned with a handful of ashes.

'See, Dalton,' Milo said, his tone gloating, and speaking before Rory had stated his opinion. 'Your lies are set to destroy you. Even your friend Billy realizes I didn't kill that doctor.'

Dalton watched Rory stomp to a halt before him and sprinkle the ashes through his fingers, shaking his head.

'No photograph,' he grunted. 'What else you got?'

Dalton took a deep breath and decided to state his full case from the beginning.

'Milo arrived here a few days ahead of Billy and the others. He came from Durando. He isn't a doctor, but he'd learnt how to save Billy's leg from a doctor, and to me that is just plain odd.'

Rory's eyes glazed on hearing such weak evidence, but he still swung round to look at Milo and requested his explanation with a bored shrug and a raised eyebrow.

'Zachary Jones was a great man,' Milo said, smiling and confident. 'There was nothing wrong with him mentioning to me how I could save a leg. Jefferson Parker would have had no choice but to chop Billy's leg off. It was lucky for him that I was here.'

Milo then paraded round on the spot smiling and possibly looking for support before he returned to stand with Eliza. Dalton wondered why he'd bothered to give such a lengthy speech, but he guessed that he'd already dismissed him as being a threat. Now, he'd seen Jefferson lose his authority and so he was showing what a reasonable and resourceful man he was so that he could perhaps one day put himself in a position where he could run the town.

But when Dalton turned to Rory, trying to think what he could say next, Rory was looking at Milo.

'You knew Doctor Zachary Jones well then, did you?' he asked.

'I did,' Milo said. 'That was why I came to you straight away when I found his dead body.'

'And he taught you how to save Billy's leg?'

'He did,' Milo said, with sudden caution in his tone.

'Odd that. Zachary Jones wasn't a sawbones. He was a dentist. Never knew nothing but how to yank out teeth.'

Milo winced when he realized he'd been caught telling a lie that Dalton had planted in his thoughts a few minutes earlier.

Dalton whooped with delight. 'I always knew your lies would destroy you, and that one was just one lie too many.'

'That was no lie,' Milo snapped, still not having regained his composure. 'I must have got two people mixed up.'

'Perhaps you did,' Rory said, taking a step towards him. 'But I'd like to hear more from the last person to see Zachary alive just as soon as someone gives me back my gun and I can arrest you.' Rory glanced at Newell. 'If that's all right with you and your town meeting.'

Newell started to nod, but Eliza spoke up.

'This is wrong,' she said. She slipped a finger under her pendant and pulled it out. 'This gold—'

'Be quiet!' Milo grunted, kneading his forehead. 'I'm trying to think.'

Milo closed his eyes, clearly realizing he'd let his veneer of calmness fall away. When Eliza looked at him aghast and Rory took another pace towards him, he roared with anger and moved to run for the nearest horse. The unarmed sheriff moved to the side to block his way and so Milo turned on his heel, looking around for support but everyone except Eliza was backing away from him quickly. So he paced towards her and grabbed her around the shoulders. He spun her round to place her back to him. A knife emerged and he pressed it against her neck.

'Nobody move,' he grunted, 'or I kill her.'

Eliza closed her eyes, perhaps more from the shock of finding that the man she'd planned to marry had turned on her than from fear. But she went limp in his grip and didn't complain as Milo backed her away from the sheriff and towards the wagon, the closest possible avenue of escape.

'Don't worry,' Dalton said to her. 'He's not taking you anywhere.'

'For once be quiet, Dalton,' Rory said. 'I'll take control of this.'

He directed everyone to give Milo plenty of room while also shooting glances at his deputies, directing them to keep watching for when Milo made a mistake. Dalton had seen the result that came when these trigger-happy lawmen were involved and he didn't move away, not believing that one of them could apprehend Milo before he could plunge in the knife. He swivelled round on his heel, watching Milo drag Eliza onto his wagon.

Milo directed Billy to get down then dragged Eliza up on to the seat and grabbed the reins. Only when Milo hurried the horse on did Dalton react. He took several long paces and hurled himself at the back of the wagon. He just caught the backboard with an outstretched hand as the wagon speeded away and then had to run and jump to keep pace with it. He felt as if his legs were falling from under him and reckoned he was in danger of falling flat on his face at any moment, but he just managed to hang on.

Ahead of the wagon the townsfolk split but one man stood before the speeding horse – Jefferson Parker. He raised a hand, warning Milo to stop.

'Stay!' he demanded. 'Prove Dalton is–'

Jefferson didn't get to finish his comment as the horse slammed into him, sending him reeling. Dalton felt a sudden lurch as the wagon trundled over Jefferson, but it did have the effect of momentarily slowing the wagon, letting Dalton loop an arm over the backboard and lift himself off the ground to hang on. Then he rolled over the board to kneel on the back of the wagon.

As he got to his feet and moved forward, he saw Milo thrust the reins into Eliza's hand and order her to drive the wagon. Then he looked back at Dalton, the knife pressed against her neck.

'Stop right there!' he grunted.

Dalton stopped walking and placed his hands palm up in a placating gesture. Milo snarled at him then nudged his head to the side, signifying that Dalton should jump off the wagon. One look at the knife convinced him he had no choice but to do as ordered. He moved to the side of the wagon aiming to vault to the ground, but then found himself losing his footing. He slipped and fell over then slammed into the other side of the wagon as Eliza steered the wagon out of the clearing and up the valley.

Dalton glanced back into the clearing to see that Rory was organizing everyone to begin a pursuit. Then they disappeared from view behind the trees. He turned back to see the sudden lurch to the side had also moved Eliza and Milo away from each other and taking advantage of the situation, Dalton jumped to his feet then threw himself forward. He slammed into Milo's back and grabbed his arm. He put his faith in the hope that no matter what Milo threatened to do he wouldn't actually stab Eliza unless it was absolutely necessary and sure enough he didn't thrust the knife at her.

When he did finally strain to move the knife towards her, Dalton already had his arm firmly held from behind. But he needed both hands to hold on and this let Milo elbow him in the guts with his free arm. The blow landed without enough force to dislodge him, but with a second lunge Milo managed to grab Dalton's jacket and yank him forward.

Dalton tumbled forward, leaning over the seat as they strained for supremacy. Dalton consoled himself with the thought that he was now sprawled over the seat between Eliza and Milo.

'Get off the wagon, Eliza,' he yelled.

She didn't follow his order but she did pull back on the reins, slowing the wagon.

'Keep going,' Milo shouted, 'or else.'

'I'm not running him down like you did Jefferson,' Eliza said.

Dalton wasn't sure what she meant and he glanced up to see that a man stood in their path. Loren had arrived. He was standing in the middle of the narrow trail, blocking their way. To the wagon's right the trail fell away followed by a slope down to the river and to the left was the treeline.

'Run him down or Dalton dies.'

'He won't get me,' Dalton grunted, although the knife was wavering dangerously close to his face.

Eliza still continued to slow the wagon, but Dalton could see that she wouldn't be able to stop it before they reached Loren who continued to stand in the middle of the trail.

'Move!' Eliza cried. Dalton echoed her cry and at the last moment Loren moved aside. Then he twirled round and with a deft manoeuvre grabbed the horse's harness then danced along at the side, helping Eliza slow the speeding wagon. Within twenty yards the combination of the slope, Loren, and Eliza brought the wagon to a halt with a lurch.

Dalton glanced up to see they'd come to a halt on the edge of the slope down to the river. While he tried to shake the knife from Milo's grasp, Loren helped Eliza down from the wagon.

Milo's eyes flared with anger as Loren climbed onto the seat, aiming to help Dalton. Loren's shadow clouded Milo's face and Dalton was sure they would have him under control within seconds, but with one last manic tug Milo dragged Dalton along the seat and over the side.

The two men hit the ground then rolled down the slope towards the river some fifty yards away, their movements uncontrolled and unstoppable. The motion shook them away from each other, leaving Dalton to tumble head over heels until he plummeted into the water.

He landed sprawling on his knees in water up to his chin. Winded and disoriented he looked around to see where Milo had come to rest but then toppled forward when Milo bundled into him. His assailant grabbed the back of his neck and drove him beneath the water. Although the water was shallow Milo still managed to submerge him and without the time to take a breath, he found himself gulping in water. Within seconds he felt his strength slipping away from him. He needed to free himself or drown.

He tried to force himself up to the surface, but Milo was standing over him and bearing all his weight down on his back to keep him beneath the water. So he did the only thing he could and forced himself downwards. This movement almost tore him from Milo's grasp when he pressed his chest to the river bottom. But Milo regained his grip by dropping down too and pressing his weight onto Dalton's back.

Dalton used the last of his strength to twist in Milo's grip. On his side he saw Milo was also below water but his bright eyes and puffed-out cheeks confirmed he'd gathered a deep breath before submerging himself and he was sure to outlast him.

Dalton had to act quickly. Already his vision was dimming and a buzzing was building in his ears. But through his rapidly darkening vision, a gleaming object on the river bottom caught his eye. He fixed his gaze on it believing it might be his last sight. The gleam made him think of the nugget he'd found that'd started off the disastrous train of events that'd led him to this situation.

Then he realized it wasn't another nugget. It was the knife. It must have come free in the struggle.

Dalton stopped struggling and went limp in Milo's hands. He felt Milo rebunch his muscles as he took a fresh hold of him. That was the chance he'd hoped for and Dalton thrust himself forward. His outstretched hand closed on the hilt and he dragged the knife back into his grasp then thrust it back and upwards, not caring where it landed, but just hoping a wild slash would find Milo's body.

Milo squirmed above him and his thrusts missed. Dalton continued to slash wildly, those parries becoming weaker as his vision darkened. He felt lighter, his actions becoming weaker and weaker.

Then suddenly he broke the surface. He'd lost the knife, but he didn't question how it'd happened and he dragged breath after breath into his grateful lungs then bent double to spew out a great torrent of water.

He stood gasping and searching around for Milo. He didn't see him at first although through his blurred vision he did see Loren picking his way down to the water's edge with Eliza in his wake. Eliza was shouting something but his ears were so full of water he couldn't hear what it was.

A shadow loomed a moment before Milo slammed into his back, again driving him forward face first into the water. He just had time to drag in a large breath and then he was underwater. Loren was only seconds away from being able to help him and Dalton reckoned he just had to prevail for a few more moments, but as he floundered he noticed that the water had a red tinge.

He fought his way back to surface and swirled round to see Milo standing before him, the knife buried in his stomach. Milo clutched his hands around it and with a great yell of pain tore it out.

He fixed his gaze on Dalton and drew back his arm, aiming to hurl it at him. Dalton rolled back on his heels then launched himself through the water, but Milo was swirling his arm forward and would release the knife before he reached him.

Then a single gunshot ripped out – Loren hitting him with deadly accuracy. Milo plummeted backwards, the knife spinning from his grasp, a red bloom exploding across his forehead before he descended beneath the water.

Several seconds later he bobbed back up to the surface, but he lay face down and by the time Loren and then Eliza waded into the water to join Dalton, he slowly drifted away towards Two Forks.

By the time Milo had disappeared from view, Eliza had nudged up close to him and in an unconscious movement that Eliza didn't object to, Dalton placed a comforting arm around her shoulders.

'I reckon Paul would have appreciated that,' Billy said.

Dalton patted the simple stone that marked Paul's grave by the side of the river. He, Loren, Eliza, and Billy had come here to commemorate his death.

The last week had been a quiet one, but after the recent chaos Dalton had enjoyed the peacefulness.

Jefferson Parker had died when Milo had run him down and even if the evidence against Milo having killed Zachary Jones had been tenuous, his wild reaction had convinced the lawman of his guilt and Billy's innocence.

Rory had left for White Falls, leaving behind a town slightly more united than it had been, although with Jefferson's demise, Dalton reckoned they stood a good chance of consolidating the steps they'd taken towards living in harmony. But for now, Dalton was more interested in his own personal friendships. To date both Loren and Eliza had been cordial, perhaps even a little shamefaced about their actions.

'Yeah,' Dalton said. 'Paul sure did want to settle down here. And I couldn't blame him. Two Forks is a fine town.'

'And you'll be stopping over in Two Forks more often now, won't you, Dalton?' Eliza asked.

'As it was you who asked, I will.' Dalton offered a smile.

'I hope...' She sighed and took a deep breath then returned the smile. 'I hope you'll be able to forgive me.'

'I don't reckon anyone has to forgive anyone about anything. Everybody did what they thought was best at the time.' Dalton looked at Loren then Eliza, receiving nods from both of them. As he reckoned most of his problems with her had started when he'd thought too much before he'd acted, he decided to just speak his mind this time. 'But as Milo had arranged a wedding for the end of the month, it'd be a shame to let those arrangements go to waste.'

Eliza's eyes opened wide, but Dalton reckoned she was more delighted than shocked.

'It would, wouldn't it?'

'Doubt there'll be time to make you a ring though.'

Eliza rubbed her neck, now free of the pendant Milo had given her.

'I've had enough of hearing about gold for now.'

'For now, but maybe...' Dalton glanced at Loren.

'Actually,' Loren said, grinning, 'if you want, we might have enough time to make a ring out of that nugget.'

Dalton looked at the river running down the valley to Two Forks, then at Billy, then at Loren, and finally at Eliza.

'No,' he said. 'Like you tried to tell me before. I have everything I need here. There ain't nothing I need that gold can give me.'

The publishers hope that this book has given you enjoyable reading. Large Print Books are especially designed to be as easy to see and hold as possible. If you wish a complete list of our books please ask at your local library or write directly to:

Dales Large Print Books
Magna House, Long Preston,
Skipton, North Yorkshire.
BD23 4ND

This Large Print Book, for people
who cannot read normal print,
is published under the auspices of

THE ULVERSCROFT FOUNDATION